D0966930

The Optician of Lampedusa

The Optician of Lampedusa

EMMA JANE KIRBY

ALLEN LANE
an imprint of
PENGUIN BOOKS

ALLEN LANE

UK | USA | Canada | Ireland | Australia
India | New Zealand | South Africa

Allen Lane is part of the Penguin Random House group of companies
whose addresses can be found at global.penguinrandomhouse.com

First published 2016
002

Set in 12/14.75 pt Dante MT Std
Typeset by Jouve (UK), Milton Keynes
Printed in Great Britain by Clays Ltd, St Ives plc

A CIP catalogue record for this book is available from the British Library

ISBN: 978–0–241–29528–1

www.greenpenguin.co.uk

Penguin Random House is committed to a sustainable future for our business, our readers and our planet. This book is made from Forest Stewardship Council® certified paper.

To my parents and to Denis

Prologue

I can hardly begin to describe to you what I saw as our boat approached the source of that terrible noise. I hardly want to. You won't understand because you weren't there. You can't understand. You see, I thought I'd heard seagulls screeching. Seagulls fighting over a lucky catch. Birds. Just birds.

We were in open sea, after all. It couldn't be anything else.

I had never seen so many people in the water. Their limbs were thrashing, hands grasping, fists punching, black faces flashing over then under the waves. Gasping, yelling, choking, screaming. Oh God, the screaming! The pitch of it! The sea boiling and writhing around them as they kicked and lashed out, clinging to each other, grabbing at pieces of driftwood, snatching handfuls of water as they tried to clutch the tops of the breakers. They were in a frenzy of desperation, shrieking at us, trying to attract our attention on the little boat. And they were scattered everywhere – in every direction I turned my head there was more of them, hundreds of them, plunging, spluttering; an outstretched arm beating the water, pleading. And my wife, sobbing my name, sobbing my name as the propeller of the motor cut a jagged, clumsy path through the bodies.

They were all drowning. I thought: how do I save them all?

I can still feel the fingers of that first hand I seized. How they cemented into mine, bone grinding against bone, how they clamped down with such a grip that I saw the sinuous veins of the wrist pounding. The force of that hold! My hand in a stranger's hand, in a bond stronger and more intimate than an umbilical cord. And my whole body shaking with the force of the hold as I pulled upwards and dragged the naked torso from the waves.

There are too many of them. Too many of them and I don't know how to do this. I'm an optician; I'm not a lifesaver. I'm an optician and I'm on holiday and I don't know how to do this.

I throw the rubber ring but there are people strewn like wreckage over a 500-metre radius and they're all crying for us. I reach out over the stern step again and again, but there are so many hands shooting out from beneath the waves, so many hands snatching at the air. My fingers lock into fingers and I pull.

Are we sinking? The boat is so low in the water now. Someone is shouting at me, but I can't stop to listen. There are too many hands. The deck is crammed with black bodies vomiting and defecating over each other. I can feel the boat protesting under the weight, rolling, ready to flip over. I know the boat is out of control.

Over there! Another hand!

I never wanted to tell you this story. I promised myself I would never tell this story again because it's not a fairy tale. There were just too many of them. I wanted to go back for them. I wanted to go back.

Do you understand what I'm trying to say to you? Maybe it's not possible for you to understand because you weren't in that boat. But I was there and I saw them. I still see them. Because it's still happening.

Chapter 1

The optician of Lampedusa is running. With each footfall, small puffs of dust rise up from the cracked road and the tiny particles swirl in a fine, rust-coloured haze around his knees. There's little wind today, even on the coastal road; it wheezes across the optician's face in dry, irregular gasps and he can smell the tang of the sea on its briny breath. It's almost too hot to be running under this glaring autumn sun, but he keeps pushing forward, the dirt clotting in patches on his legs as it mingles with his sweat. Somewhere, perhaps from the port at the mouth of the town, he can hear a dog howling. Whatever time of day or night on this island, he thinks, there's always a stray dog barking somewhere.

It's more Africa than Italy really. Running here, away from the gelato and cappuccino bars and the souvenir shops of the little town, you could imagine you were in Africa, especially when you passed a little stone-walled *dammuso* with its white-washed roof. He screws up his eyes. You can almost see the African coast from here. Tunisia, Lampedusa's nearest neighbour, is twice as close as Sicily.

Twenty-five years he has lived in this dry, arid landscape now. For twenty-five years he has been running through this craggy, barren scrubland, getting scratched by its thorn bushes and caked with its grime. So different – this calm – from the agitated chaos of his native Naples, but the optician has never regretted exchanging his sprawling city for the solitude of this little island. It may be only ten square kilometres long, perhaps half the size of Naples, but with Lampedusa, he's got sea on all sides. The optician needs the sea.

He's looking at the water now as he jogs along the tracks of the island's south coast. Splintered cobalt and turquoise as bright and smooth as cheap jewellery and he knows that if he were to dive into it now, even though today is the first day of October, it would still be warm and welcoming. Out on the boat with his wife Teresa, he watches dolphins and sometimes sperm whales swimming in the tranquil waters. They often swim themselves at the paradisiacal Rabbit Beach where the bleached sands radiate heat and occasional shoals of parrotfish splash colour across the white canvas as they flit and dart across the bay in the fractured light. In the summer, the rare loggerhead turtles choose these beaches to lay their eggs. His wife says it's because Nature recognizes that Lampedusa will always be gentle with whatever washes up here.

The optician's feet pound on. The heat has caused a knotted vein just above his right ear to pulse and he can trace it throbbing across his bald head and up into his skull. He likes to push himself, to feel his body working. He's always been slim and fit. Years ago, he'd enjoyed the physical discipline of his military service, and although he might be in his late fifties now, he won't let anything slip.

A teenager roars past him on an old scooter, the rowdy engine shattering the silence of his run. He watches the boy weaving pointless tyre trails in and out of the dust, wheeling and revving the bike. There's not much for the youth to do here in the evenings – a handful of bars and cafés, a small nightclub with a karaoke machine. His own parents hadn't wanted him hanging around Naples when he'd left school – getting bored and into trouble. They'd sent him to a tailoring college where he'd learnt how to cut made-to-measure suits. He'd become famous for his exactness and precision. He smiles to himself. He knew it was never really going to satisfy him in the long term though, not when he was nurturing a secret ambition to become an optician. A strange passion for a young man, you might think, but he has always been fascinated by sight, by how and what people see. So alongside his tailoring, he studied optics.

A small group of African men are shuffling towards him down the road into town. He lifts a hand as he passes them and they mutter a shy greeting in return. He wonders if they have arrived on the island that morning – almost every day now he sees the buses leaving the port packed with newly arrived migrants. They hang out by the supermarket opposite his shop and he sees crowds of them cluster around the church. Maybe they're very Christian in whatever part of Africa they come from? His neighbours collect food and stuff for them; there's always someone rattling a tin. A woman, presumably from the parish, had called round this morning, asking if he had any old clothes or shoes to donate, but he'd been drowning in paperwork and hadn't had time to stop. Apparently the migrant centre is bursting again; maybe that's why they prefer to wander the island like this.

Crazy, he thinks, that they all turn up here when this country has precious little to offer them. There had been many a moment over the last few years when he thought his own business was going under; how many sleepless nights have he and Teresa had over that? He exhales noisily. Everything he had worked so damn hard for threatened! He feels his heart rate increase to keep pace with his rising temper. The town hall here was constantly yanking up the business rates until he was half strangled by taxes and fees and duties and God knows what else. It feels as if he is always being hounded and tapped for money by some official or other.

He's facing into the low sun here and it's staring him out.

He sees little coloured sparks of red and gold and green when he blinks and he puts a hand up to shield himself from the glare. He should have worn sunglasses. The lights flash and fizz around his eyes.

He worries for his two sons mostly, of course. He needs to make sure they're provided for, because frankly how on earth they'll find long-term jobs in this shrinking economy he does not know. They're bright lads, both of them, and hard workers too. The eldest wants to set up his own business; he's got a real entrepreneurial spirit, that one, but of course it's a risk. Being self-employed is always risky, as he knows all too well.

But he could not imagine working for anyone else now; it would be unthinkable. His gaze sweeps from left to right. Being master of himself, his own time, managing his own little world – that's what he likes. And no one could say he doesn't put the hours in; he works hard during the week keeping his little business thriving for the family, and then his reward – he looks back over his shoulder towards the sea again – is having all this wonderful nature as his own playground.

The seagulls have begun mewing excitedly and the optician looks upwards to watch them flock and circle over the coast. He knows they're waiting for the last of the fishing trawlers to head back to port, hoping to pick up scraps. If he can time his run right, he'll be back at the port in time to meet the boat and will get the pick of the catch for supper.

He jogs past some young Africans crouched on the roadside, fiddling with their mobile phones. He nods to them politely and they watch him curiously as he thunders on in his sweat-soaked T-shirt. The scrub behind them is strewn with coloured food wrappers and squashed drink cartons. He kicks a can to the edge of the road. So much rubbish on the island now! Bits of blue plastic sheeting snagged on the thorn bushes, old food boxes everywhere.

Twenty years ago, when he could run the island's roads effortlessly, the optician of Lampedusa would sometimes spot a scared migrant scrambling up the rocks onto his path. They had almost always been alone and would shout to him in English: 'Where am I? Am I in Palermo? Have I reached Sicily?'

He shakes his head in disbelief. It seems a long time ago now. The Arab Spring changed everything and they never come on their own any more. Big boatloads arrive now in a constant stream – whole families; women and children too, poor things. Only a couple of years ago, the newspapers were reporting that Lampedusa now had more migrants and refugees than inhabitants! The skin on his forehead wrinkles. Best not to think too much about it really. The TV, the papers – they're saturated with news about migrants; it's all they talk about. There was something else on the radio the other day about some more drowning off the coast of Sicily. Seven or eight of them, was it?

He breaks his stride to let a scrawny cat slink across the road in front of him and watches it hunker down in the thorn bushes. Of course, he had moved here to get away from Naples really. In the 1980s Naples seemed vacuous: mindless political rows, nothing profound; he'd felt his points of reference were just slipping away. This small island, though, had been the perfect place to construct a new and more meaningful life. It was impossible not to feel anchored in this natural beauty – the buttery limestone cliffs offering those idyllic sandy beaches at their base, and then the harsh wildness of the north of the island that he found so empowering.

There's laughter suddenly and two middle-aged men, laden with binoculars and expensive-looking cameras, appear from the bank just in front of him. They're speaking Italian, but he can hear they're not local – bird-watchers from Milan most probably; most of the tourists seem to be from Milan. They're excited and animated and the younger man calls to him that they've just spotted some rare breed of wading bird whose name the optician doesn't catch. He turns inland.

Now that the season's over, there are very few tourists around, but it's been a quiet summer altogether. The migrants, he thinks, are hardly a positive tourist attraction and many holidaymakers have chosen Sardinia over Lampedusa for their annual break this year. Friends in the hotel and catering trades have complained to him about the drop in takings. Good job his own business is not reliant on the tourist trade.

At the entrance to the island's graveyard, a grey-haired man in a bright blue polo shirt is hunched over a bench, drilling breeze-blocks. The concrete slabs spit out sparks as he works and the optician wonders vaguely what he's making so intently. The crosses on top of the bevelled mausoleums glint in the early evening light.

He's on the homeward stretch now and feeling positive. Tomorrow he's awarding himself a couple of days off to take a boat trip with his wife and some close friends. It'll be good to switch off for a bit, to stop worrying about the accounts, about the boys' futures and just to watch the open sea roll out before him, with all its vastness and possibilities. He looks up at the cloudless sky and his thin lips stretch into a grin. Promising weather.

His friend Francesco would have spent the morning polishing *Galata*, scrubbing her royal blue and brick-red hull, sprucing her up for her imminent outing. He smiles indulgently. Good old Francesco! They'd had some laughs on that boat over the years. Francesco treated her as if she were a luxury yacht rather than a tarted-up 15-metre wooden fishing boat. He kept the white paint of her wheelhouse immaculate.

There's already a small queue at the fishmonger's on the harbour front. Laid out on the crushed-ice trays are blue-fin tuna, round-bellied *sardinella* and huge, long-billed swordfish. A shop worker is helping the last of the fishermen to unload his catch of bruise-coloured squid, the purple, jellied tentacles spilling over the side of the box.

Last push up the hill now, and then on to the Via Roma to his little flat above the shop for a shower. On his left, beached in a huge car park, are the jumbled wrecks of wooden boats that have brought migrants to the island from Libya. Tipped awkwardly onto their sides, their cracked hulls are blistered with cheerful turquoise and ox-blood paint.

But the optician has other things on his mind. Right now, he's hungry and he wants to shower and to buy some sardines at the portside for supper with his wife. He needs to call his friend Matteo about what supplies to pack for their boating trip and to work out who's bringing the wine. It should be a fun trip with all eight of them out on the water together.

Perhaps, if the wind had suddenly picked up spirit that night, as it so often does in Lampedusa, and had begun to thrash the little fishing boats against the harbour sea wall and to needle the sea until it raged in fury, the optician would never have boarded his friend's little pleasure boat and would never have cast off. He would have simply postponed his trip and gone out with his friends for *aperitivo* at the usual bar, then maybe on to dinner at one of the local restaurants. He would have been disappointed, irritated perhaps, and in the morning at his shop, when a customer choosing new frames for his glasses politely asked him what he had been up to lately, he would have shrugged and replied frankly, that he had nothing to tell.

But the wind stayed soft. And he did cast off.

Chapter 2

The door leading to the apartment was open when he arrived back at the shop. He hated that. He hated it when the lines between work and private life got blurred. Customers were so nosey when they heard the door creak open and saw Teresa coming downstairs; they always craned their necks to try to see inside the door, to get a glimpse of how the optician and his wife lived. It irritated him how fascinated people were by the private living arrangements of others.

He closed the door firmly and jogged up the stairs, where he found Teresa in the sitting room reading a magazine.

'The door was open again,' he said pointedly. She smiled vaguely and looked up briefly from her reading.

'Was it, dear?' she asked, playing with the thick strands of her blonde hair. 'Oh well.'

The sitting room was hot with the day's sunshine and Teresa had left the window open wide. The pages of the novel he'd been reading yesterday fluttered a little in the light breeze and he picked up the book and flattened it between his palms, carefully running his thumb down the spine before slotting it back into the weathered wooden bookcase. He'd like to replace the furniture in here one day soon; it was all getting a little tired-looking, especially the glass coffee table which was scored and scratched all over. It made him wince to see the damaged glass.

He went into the little kitchen, took the tumbler that was standing on the draining board and poured himself a large glass of water from the bottle in the fridge. He knocked it back quickly and poured himself another with which he wandered back to the doorway of the sitting room. His wife had been right to insist they got that chap to paint up here as well when they'd redecorated the shop last year. The white walls made the place look clean and bigger than it was.

'I thought I'd get sardines for supper,' he said, addressing the back of his wife's head. 'I saw the boat come in.'

Teresa craned her neck to look at him, wrinkling her nose. 'Aren't you going to shower, dear?' she replied.

Under the shower he thought about what he needed to pack for the trip tomorrow. Were his apple-green swimming shorts clean? He'd rather take them than the new navy ones his youngest son had given him for his birthday. Things got torn on boats. On that last trip they'd taken with Francesco in the summer, he'd ripped his windcheater on the corner of the table in the cabin; he had mended it carefully, restitching the pocket so that you couldn't really tell it had ever been otherwise, but the fact was, he knew that it was damaged and it annoyed him to think of it even now.

He liked to be careful with his things. He'd pack the new pair of fake Converse that he'd picked up at the Naples market – it wouldn't be a tragedy if they got salt-stained. He smiled to himself. They were the same dark grey as Matteo's, except his had cost fifteen euros whereas Matteo's had set him back over sixty! He could still see Matteo's stunned face when he'd told him last week. His friend had bent down and examined them, checked the soles, rubbed the cotton tongue between his finger and thumb and cursed. He chuckled as the hot water ran down his back. He enjoyed getting one over on that young upstart! It always felt good to teach the young ones a trick or two. Not that Matteo was exactly a spring chicken any more; he had already said goodbye to forty, but Matteo did love to rib him about his impending sixtieth. Cheeky beggar called Francesco 'Grandad!'

He looked at himself in the mirror as he towelled himself dry. You had to admit he wasn't doing badly for a man in his late fifties. There was no spare flesh on him really and his stomach had resisted developing a middle-aged paunch. He flexed his chest muscles and saw the sinews stretch. It wasn't about vanity, this keeping fit business. He just didn't like to let himself go. Discipline. You got nowhere in life without discipline. It was what he'd always repeated to his sons during their early teenage years, when they had just wanted to laze around the house with headphones on like zombies. Discipline and damn hard work. That's what you needed if you wanted to get somewhere, he had told his boys while they rolled their eyes at him and pretended to drop off to sleep in boredom. He peered at an age spot on his bald forehead. Mind you, the message had filtered through those headphones of theirs somehow or other. He was proud of them both, he really was. He loved to talk about them to Gabriele and Francesco, to show them the latest photos. He was careful, though, not to sound boastful; no one likes a show-off. He grinned in the mirror. He had good teeth.

There was a small canvas bag on the bed; Teresa must have already packed her stuff. He made a mental note to remind her to bring a fleece or a warm sweater; it was bright sunshine now all right, but early October could be fickle with its winds. He'd pack in the morning. He was in a hurry to get back down to the port and get those sardines before someone else snaffled them. He would never buy them if there was only a scattering left in the tray; he always suspected that the fishmonger bulked them out with a few of the previous day's leftover catch when stocks ran low. Buying fish was very much his job; Teresa never seemed to notice when the sardines looked tired or dry. She trusted everyone, his wife did. Always giving people the benefit of the doubt.

He picked up from the bed the white shirt he'd been wearing this morning and flicked at a bit of grime around the right cuff. It would do for tonight, for frying sardines. He heard the phone ring as he put on his shirt and as soon as he heard his wife's giggles he guessed it was Maria on the other end. Those two together! Thick as thieves. Teresa was calling to him from the sitting room. Maria fancied dinner out tonight, she said, to mark the start of our holiday. Giulia's coming too and Gabriele – shall we join them?

He checked his watch. It was touch and go whether he'd make the fishmonger's now. He hesitated; he hated changing plans. Oh well, why not! Teresa would love it and it would be a good way to sort out who was bringing what for the boat trip tomorrow rather than sending round umpteen texts. Besides, it would give him an hour or so downstairs to make sure everything was in order in the shop before they went away on their little break.

'Fine!' he called through the door. 'But not that awful place Matteo chose last week – the electric light in there is offensive!'

Before he went downstairs he changed out of the white shirt and slipped the clean black one from the hanger that was hooked onto the back of the bedroom door. It smelled of lavender and vaguely of Teresa.

He stretched out at the top of the stairs, touching his hands to the floor and bouncing them there for a few moments. He fancied he could hear his spine creaking: he'd have to see about it one of these days. Stiffness in the back was a hazard of the job – you spent half your day as an optician twisting and bent over retinoscopes and ophthalmoscopes, and the other half crouched at a desk doing the paperwork.

Teresa had filled the jug behind the counter with some big paper sunflowers and he was surprised he hadn't noticed when he'd walked into the shop after his run. He sized them up suspiciously, wondering if they weren't a little garish. No, on balance Teresa was right. Their bright yellow was clean and cheery and somehow made the shop look less clinical. It may not feel like it now, but autumn would creep up quickly on Lampedusa. The sky would turn sour and mouldy and then they would need every bit of help they could get to lure people through the doors if they were to shift last season's sunglasses.

He picked up the diary to check that Teresa had cancelled all his appointments for the next couple of days. He saw she had highlighted a name in pink for next Wednesday. Oh yes, Mrs Maggiorani. She always needed a courtesy call the night before to remind her she had an appointment.

Unbelievable, really, that some people led such muddled lives! He was a list-maker. Every day he made a neat list of tasks he had to do and goals he wanted to achieve and every evening he ticked them off. That way you kept track, you kept on top of things. He rubbed out a line in the diary reminding him to chase up the lab for Mr Esposito's bifocals; he'd done that this morning from his mobile while he was on hold on the landline to a supplier in Naples. You had to show life very clearly who was boss, who was in command, or life would quickly take advantage and wreak havoc.

He leafed through the mail to see if there was anything that Teresa had left outstanding. There was that thank-you letter she had told him about over lunch from the old lady in Turin. He'd fixed her glasses back in early September when she'd come over for a holiday to see her sister. She'd dropped them off a balcony and was so distraught when she'd come in to see him because she couldn't read without them. It had taken him a couple of days to sort them out and to find the right lens, but he'd fixed her up with something else to be getting along with. She had been stunned when he'd said there was no charge. He'd had all the stuff in the shop anyway so it wasn't a problem and she was a nice old dear. Honest, she called him in her letter, lovely to meet such an honest man. He smiled to himself. Not often you heard a man from Naples being described as honest. That had been one of the reasons he had left, actually; he just couldn't bear being tainted with the same overtones of double-dealing and corruption that he felt his home city stank of.

You had to be trustworthy as an optician. There was an intimacy about his job, about peering right inside someone's eyeball, your face just inches from his or hers. At the beginning of his studies, his father had worried that he might be too shy for such close contact with strangers, but he had found it easy to be polite, then to distance himself, breaking down the person into retina, blood vessels and optic nerves. Funnily enough, Teresa often told him nowadays that he had a tendency to stare at people when he was out with them, as if he was examining them and boring down into their eyeballs. A tic of the job, he supposed, a habit. She'd nudge him under the table when he was doing it; it made people uncomfortable, she said, to feel as if they were under the microscope when they were trying to have dinner.

Right. What else was left to do? He looked over at the display case containing the contact lenses and solutions. No, that was all well stocked, although – how had that happened? – someone had put a green bottle of saline solution on the shelf that was for the blue gas-permeable products. He rearranged the shelf correctly, frowning.

Teresa came downstairs and handed him his black jacket. Time to go, she said. She was wearing the long silver necklace he liked, the one with the intertwining strands which she fiddled with when she was nervous. Her blonde hair spilled over the shoulders of her silky grey top. It was still as thick and copious as it had been when he'd first met her as a fourteen-year-old schoolgirl.

'Maria has booked the restaurant on the little hill overlooking the port,' she said. He opened his mouth to speak.

'The one you like,' she added, firmly taking his arm.

Before he flicked off the light switch, he moved the men's sunglasses stand an inch or two to the right so that it was symmetrical with the women's stand opposite.

His own street was Lampedusa's commercial hub: a wide pedestrianized boulevard with polished grey flagstones that shone under the electric light of the street lamps. It was really the only place on the island for the evening *passeggiata* and was peppered with wooden benches, smart cafés and boutiques. Lampedusa had never gone in for high-rise; almost all the apartment blocks and shops on the street were only two or three storeys high and they were pressed close together in terraces to make the best use of space. Most of the houses' façades were the rich cream colour of the local lime plaster. Others had had a modern makeover and sported walls in shades of lemon, sulphur and mustard. Behind Via Roma, the streets were narrower and shabbier. There was always building work taking place on the island, always some house or apartment standing bare and unrendered. He'd lost track of which buildings were actually being constructed or renovated and which had just been abandoned to crumble into the ground. A neighbour called good evening to them from her balcony as they headed to the port, peeping over the top of some bed sheets that were drying on her washing line.

The season may have been over but the restaurant was packed. They were lucky Maria was able to get a table. He sat next to Giulia, who as usual was battling to tame her frizz of hair. She was torturing her curls into an elastic band behind her head as she greeted him, swearing as one of those dangly turtle earrings she always wore got caught up and imprisoned in the mass of hair. She looked tired, he thought. It was a busy time of year for Giulia and her partner Gabriele; they were packing up their beach accessories shop for the winter, going through stock that needed to be sold off, and sorting storage for items that would keep for when they reopened in March. If they reopened in March, she muttered. The business rents were soaring so fast you had to be a millionaire to keep up with them. She and the optician raised their eyebrows at one another.

Where was the wine? Maria was asking, looking around for the waiter. Gabriele had ordered the Sicilian red, but the optician was sceptical and had asked for a small glass to taste first. Maria would be closing up her swimsuit boutique for the winter soon and heading back to Catania; he could hear her telling the girls to pop by over the next couple of weeks if they wanted a look in before she put the costumes on general sale. Her neck was draped with a long gold scarf that was crocheted like fishing nets. He recognized it as the one Teresa had pointed out to him in her shop window last week. Maria always had on something different. He looked at her fondly. He liked that she took risks with her clothes; that she dared to be maverick. Teresa was much more classic, he thought as he watched his wife play with the strands of her silver necklace. But Teresa carried off classic beautifully. She had class, his wife did.

He laughed at Gabriele, who was holding the menu far away from his face, peering as he tried to decipher what was written on it. He nudged Maria to look too.

'Admit you're getting as old as the rest of us!' Maria teased him.

'And go and see our bald friend here and get your beautiful blue eyes fitted with some glasses!'

He was a serious chap, Gabriele, and his domed forehead made him look even more so. Dependable was how Teresa always described him and she was right. If ever he had had to go to Sicily or to Naples on an overnight work trip, Gabriele would be sure to swing by to make sure Teresa was OK on her own.

The red wine was thin and lacked generosity. He ordered the white.

The women were admiring Elena's new hairstyle. She had added a thick streak of blonde in her dark fringe. Less accountant, more Lampedusa, she joked, flicking back her long hair over her shoulder. She clowned a sad face. She was dreading leaving the sunshine and the big wide skies of the island to return to the cramped, dull finance office in the north of Italy where she worked during the winter months.

She made a grab for the bottle of wine. *Buone vacanze*! she gasped, filling her glass to the brim and slurping the wine like a desperate alcoholic. They all laughed.

He and Teresa sat out the *primo piatto*; they were careful not to eat too many carbohydrates in the evening. The waiter brought him the platter of sea bream and swordfish to inspect and he considered them carefully, asking for precise details of exactly where and when they'd been caught. He listened intently to the waiter's replies, his gaze probing the man's perspiring face. He felt Teresa giving him a warning tug on his jacket. He chose the sea bream. The eyes on the swordfish looked a little milky.

Giulia exchanged a private look with Teresa, who giggled surreptitiously behind her sleeve. He looked at them, feigning hurt.

'How does she put up with you?' Giulia mocked. 'Mr Fastidious!' He threw his hands in the air.

Matteo would soon be heading back to the mainland too, Maria told them over the fish (which incidentally was very good; they all had to agree he had made the right choice). It had been a bad year for Matteo workwise, a real struggle to get a job, she was saying. And Francesco had had a call from the workshop this morning, she added. He and his carpentry skills were needed back in Milan by the end of the month, much earlier than he would have liked. He'd have to leave his daughter running the ice-cream parlour alone for a bit. They all groaned in sympathy. No one liked leaving the island.

He took out his tobacco pouch and began to roll himself a cigarette. One after a meal was the limit. Just the one. He excused himself from the table.

There was still no sign of a wind outside and the air, although warm, was losing its sweet scent of summer. He could hear the gentle clinking of the boats as the sea teased them away from their chains, and he knew that somewhere out there in the dark *Galata* was waiting for them. He'd have a look at the maritime forecast when he got home. He knew that Francesco would have already checked, but he'd have a look anyway. A wind this warm and light could mean the treacherous Sirocco was on its way. It blew in stealthily from the Sahara, picking up speed across Libya, roaring its way over the Mediterranean until it burst open on Sicily and Lampedusa. And when the Sirocco came, that's when you knew autumn was on its way too, prompting half the islanders to pack up, turn about and sit out the winter on the mainland.

He extinguished his cigarette. It was a funny time of year, October. The beginning of the end, really.

Chapter 3

The optician of Lampedusa stretched out lazily in his bunk and felt the first tentative shafts of early morning light play across his face, teasing him out of slumber. The swell underneath the boat rocked him gently into consciousness and into the delicious realization that he was on holiday and that today no one was going to badger him about broken frames or complain about scratched lenses. He sighed contentedly. Such peace. Everyone else on board was still asleep. As he set the water boiling for his coffee, he could already hear the first seagulls squabbling.

Up on the deck, feeling a little chilly in the dawn dampness, the optician clutched his coffee cup and zipped up the collar of his navy windcheater as he watched the fledgling sunrise. The wind was light, it was barely tickling the water, and the sun, as it rose higher and hotter, would have no bother pushing away the few light clouds that were currently pestering the new sky. It looked to be a glorious morning for a pleasure cruise and a spot of fishing. A ripple of childish excitement pulsated through him. How he loved the sea! The immensity of it! He'd always found being on the water so restorative and being with his close friends out here, well, that was about as good as it got.

They'd had a laugh last night! Old Francesco was such a good raconteur after a glass or two, his grey ponytail stiff with salt, looking like a seasoned country and western star as he told his tall tales. Matteo egged him on mercilessly. Poor Gabriele had been ribbed all day – mind you, it made a change for the optician himself not to be the butt of all the jokes – they were always teasing him about being so finicky and precise, wanting everything done just so in a very particular way.

He grinned to himself. Gabriele fancied himself quite the fisherman, yet he'd been the only one of the boys not to contribute a single fish to the supper pail. They'd watched him getting more and more irritated as another fish was landed and dropped in the bucket – time and time again he'd reeled in his line, checked the bait, sighed huffily and recast. He had no idea, his rod being on the other side of the boat, that Matteo had been teasing him by repeatedly slapping down the same fish in the bucket. Matteo's supposed good fortune had driven Gabriele's competitive spirit into overdrive – Maria and Teresa were doubled up, clutching each other and biting their lips to stop the sound of their laughter giving the game away.

It had been great to see Teresa let herself go like that. She was such a worrier, but she always relaxed around Maria – everyone did really. You couldn't meet a warmer woman; she was always clucking round, making sure that everyone was happy and feeling included without ever overstepping the mark into irritating do-gooder territory. He smiled indulgently. Great softie! It was Maria who'd called time on the prank with Gabriele; she couldn't bear to see him made a fool of.

He'd gone nuts though, Gabriele, when he'd clocked the joke – leaping on top of Matteo, knocking him to the floor, trying to slap his bearded face with the offending fish and then tussling and struggling with him on the deck until they'd both slid off the stern steps and plummeted into the sea. Giulia had filmed some of it on her smartphone camera – when they'd watched the video later, the images had been about as smooth as if she'd been filming in a force nine gale – she'd been laughing so much that she couldn't hold the phone still.

They'd all ended up in the sea afterwards. One by one

they'd dived in, whooping like children, splashing each other, chasing the last light of the evening before the sun sank and its fiery colours fizzled out as it hit the waterline. The autumn chill was yet to spoil the water; it was still 21 °C and mucking around in it with his friends, the optician could sense again the optimism of summer. What was it Elena had said when she was floating beside him, her long dark hair fanning out around her head? That swimming in the autumn was like a rebirth. If you got a few good swims behind you in October, you felt renewed and ready to face the winter ahead.

He'd stayed in for a little while after the others had climbed out and were hosing themselves down on the boat's steps. It was wonderful to be in the darkening velvety warmth, to let the swell take his body and push and nudge it wherever it pleased, its rhythmic music accompanied by the tinkling laughter of his friends.

It had been so deliciously peaceful and welcoming. He'd almost felt guilty when he'd started swimming; it seemed barbaric somehow to churn up this glassy water with all that kicking and chopping. So he'd stroked through it very gently, barely troubling the surface like a polite and courteous guest tiptoeing through a house at night so as not to disturb his host.

Yes, he was grateful to the sea all right. Its salt was still tight on his skin from yesterday's swim. Changed your ideas, the sea did. Made you see things more clearly, more positively somehow – all that calmness. Although, he thought with a tiny pang of annoyance, it would be even better if those seagulls would tone it down a bit.

His coffee was almost cold now. He drained the cup and wondered whether he should fetch another or enjoy the last few moments of solitude before the others came up on deck. He could already feel someone stirring in the cabin below. He stretched and rolled his head slowly in a circle, listening to his neck crack. He deserved this holiday really and he wanted to savour every little golden moment of it.

But something was niggling him. There was something about the way the seagulls were mewing that had him on edge. It was the pitch of the damned birds. Never satisfied, always complaining or bickering and picking petty squabbles with each other. His skin prickled with irritation.

Matteo came up on deck, shirtless, his arms and chest criss-crossed with a dark pattern of intertwined tattoos. His finger was in the air, his face concentrated in listening. He didn't pause to wish his friend good morning.

'Do you hear it?' Matteo asked the optician urgently. 'There's something out there.'

The optician trained his ear to the sound. 'It's not seagulls?' he asked. 'Seagulls screaming?'

Gabriele and Francesco joined them. 'Something is screaming,' Gabriele confirmed slowly, 'But I don't think it's seagulls, do you, Francesco?'

Francesco held the cold metal gunwale of his boat and concentrated. It didn't make sense, this sound.

The men stood silent for a long moment and peered across the water at the barely imperceptible cat's paw prints on the surface. As the women hurried from their bunks and rocked the cabin below, a few small waves slapped across the boat's hull and the mewling noise was lost for a few seconds. The sea shushed and calmed itself, but almost immediately the wind threw back the eerie sound again, a sort of animalistic baying.

The optician shuddered involuntarily. 'What is it?' he whispered. 'What's out there?'

His eyes darted nervously around the boat. There were no other vessels on the water. Aside from the sinister intermittent shrieking, they were on their own.

But Francesco had already started the engine.

As the men pulled up the anchor, the women scrambled up onto the deck.

'What's going on? What's that awful noise?'

His wife Teresa sounded panicky – she was easily flustered and upset by sudden problems. She was fifty now, yet she'd never really shrugged off her childish sense of innocence and wonder. It made her very endearing; practically everyone she had ever met had wanted to protect her. But the optician often worried that her openness also left her vulnerable. He sometimes told her she needed to toughen up.

'We're sorting it,' he promised her as soothingly as he could. 'We're going to take a look. Yell if you see something, girls.'

'But it sounds like something is really suffering,' she insisted. 'It sounds like something's in pain.' She held the edge of his windcheater and looked up at him anxiously.

'We're sorting it!' the optician replied firmly.

Teresa, Maria and Elena took up lookout posts at the bow. Freed of her anchor, *Galata* chugged out of the mouth of the protected cove and into the open sea. Waves hit with greater force against the boat's hull and the optician checked his watch mechanically – it was just after six o clock. He swung himself up onto the roof of the cabin to get a clearer view of the water. But whatever was out there, the sea, dutifully reflecting back the orange sky, was giving no clues.

Matteo and Gabriele paced the little boat impatiently, swearing under their breath. The women were silent at their posts, breathing heavily and locked in fear. The optician's wife gripped Elena's arm.

The motorboat's outboard engine sliced easily through the water, leaving behind a trail of frothing backwash that split into two like a whale's fin. Yesterday afternoon the optician had sat at the stern for a good half-hour, transfixed by the hypnotic regularity of the wake, his mind lulled and comforted by the continually splitting vortex. Now he watched the disturbed water nervously and his finger worried at the pulsating vein on his right temple.

'See anything?' Matteo shouted up to him.

He shook his head and the two men exchanged looks of bafflement at each other.

He couldn't hear the damned noise any more. Were they even on the right course now? He whistled to Gabriele and when he looked up, he tapped both his ears in an exaggerated mime of deafness. Gabriele yelled down to Francesco to cut the engine and its throaty roar petered out and died.

Galata shuddered spasmodically in the water from the brutal braking, lurching and trembling. Her crew, motionless, waited for the sea to settle. Maria leant over and took Teresa's other arm. Giulia, standing a little apart from the others, was biting the knuckles of her right hand, her left struggling to pull back her rebellious hair behind her neck. How vulnerable they looked, the four of them. He was alarmed for them, but he couldn't show it.

When it came this time, the monstrous, tortured howl ripped through everyone like a bullet. Instinctively, the optician moved his hand to protect his face. He staggered to keep his footing on the cabin roof. What the hell was out there?

The howl mutated into an unbearable screeching. The optician felt his stomach knot. Something was roaring underneath the waves and whatever it was the optician had a gut feeling that when they found it, it would be truly terrible. He forced himself to regulate his breathing and tried to nod reassuringly at Teresa who was looking at him in horror.

Then, suddenly he saw it. 'Fish! I see three big fish there! Francesco – five o'clock!'

Francesco manoeuvred the boat to follow his outstretched arm. The optician kept his eye trained on the black dots he had seen bobbing on the water and tried to steady his mind. But his brain was arguing with his eyes. What kind of fish would be on the surface of the water, idiot? Come on, what kind of fish?

'More fish there!' Maria was pointing slightly to the right of his outstretched arm, leaning over the rail, face screwed up against the sun. But the optician was still staring with a professional intensity at the objects he had spotted, focused as fixedly as a customer in his own shop when sitting in front of the reading charts. He willed his eyes and brain to recognize and interpret the forms.

Galata drifted closer, the little boat dancing nervously up and down in the slight swell. They were thirty metres away and the frenetic clamouring was intensifying.

The optician started. One of the black shapes he was watching lengthened, partly lifted up from the water and flopped down again into a ball. It disappeared, leaving a white froth of disturbed water.

Oh God, no. Please God, no.

'People!' Giulia screamed. 'There are people in the water!'

Standing high above the water level on the cabin roof, his arm still outstretched, the optician saw the black dots come into focus. Bodies were flung like skittles across the sea's glassy surface, some bobbing precariously, some horizontal and horribly heavy. The people in the water had all seen *Galata* now and they were churning the sea into a frenzy with their flailing arms and legs. Every time a wave collapsed, another black dot or head was revealed. The sea was littered with them.

The ocean resonated with the primitive screaming, the terrible sound bouncing off and under the water, gargling and rupturing. The optician recognized it as the music of the dying, the final dirge of the drowning, played out right in front of their boat. And through the chorus of voices he could pick out each individual soloist. Everyone was begging to be noticed.

The optician swallowed. How, he thought, how do I save them all? He lowered his outstretched arm slowly. In the water, hands snatched despairingly upwards, clutching at air, reaching futilely towards him. He could see yellowing eyes staring wild and wide at him, frantic at the hope of salvation.

He glanced down at his friends on deck. Eight. There were eight of them and there were scores, no, hundreds of people in the water. And they had just one rubber ring.

Even before he jumped down from the cabin and back onto the deck, the optician had understood that he would have to choose who would live and who would die.

Chapter 4

There had been no arguments about who should give orders, not a second wasted with debate over who should perform what function, who should stand where. Matteo, without hesitating, had simply dived into the water and started scooping and dragging people towards the boat. Gabriele raced into the cockpit and gave the pan-pan emergency call on the radio, relieving Francesco at the wheel.

The optician was sweating even before Matteo had hauled the first spluttering man to the boat's stern. He'd thrown off his windcheater and he could feel the blood pumping through his chest and limbs, his body quarrying adrenalin as he stood on the wooden decking of the step. His muscles itched to be used and his breathing was impatient.

The first man they pulled from the sea had slipped back under. He looked barely more than a boy. The optician and Francesco had hauled him up by his wrists, but the young chap was completely naked, covered in diesel and as slippery as a fish. When he'd resurfaced again, spluttering and crying, it had been difficult to find purchase on the oily flesh that was as smooth and polished as an aubergine. The optician's nails bit into the dark skin as he yanked him aboard. He'd never held anyone's hand so tightly before – the intimacy of the gesture with a naked total stranger had made him wince. And yet when the force of the pull had flung the man against his bare chest, he'd felt something strangely primeval stir in him, something almost like love. He'd wanted to hold the adolescent, to hug him to him in the same way he had done with his own sons when they were frightened or in trouble.

But there wasn't time for emotion. Matteo was already yelling for help with the next survivor and was struggling to free himself from him; his head intermittently forced underwater as the drowning man clutched at his neck and scrabbled with his feet, trying to hook his legs around Matteo's tattooed torso. All around the boat, from every direction, voices shrieked in panic.

'You'll be fine, you'll be fine!' the optician shouted to the young man over his shoulder, wiping the oil from his own hands onto his trousers. 'We're going to save your friends now – don't worry!'

On the deck, the teenager had instantly rolled into a foetal ball, vomiting seawater and shaking so hard the women thought he might be fitting. He was weeping and moaning to himself in a language that they didn't understand.

He screamed, though, when Maria touched his shoulder and had jerked backwards, covering his private parts with his trembling hands. Sensitive Teresa understood his shame immediately and dashed below deck to get her weekend bag. The first thing she pulled from the canvas was a vermilion-coloured T-shirt and he snatched it from her to hide himself. He put his legs through the armholes and wore the T-shirt like a giant pair of underpants or a nappy, knotting the material at the side. He sobbed like a baby, rocking himself.

There was a question that needed to be asked, although the optician was not sure he was ready for the answer. He steeled himself.

'How many of you were on the boat?' he urged, counting on his fingers to indicate numbers. The exhausted teenager leant forward and with his finger traced a figure on the deck – 500. The optician's mouth fell open. The young man leant forward again and added a symbol: +.

Three men were now on board and Gabriele was manoeuvring the boat towards the next little group. Everyone had seemed to understand implicitly that they had to focus their rescue efforts on the clusters of survivors, rather than on lone individuals; no one had protested when they'd let a corpse smack back down under the quartzy surface. The teamwork had been second to none really, a factory conveyor belt, saving, sorting and securing. It was as if, thought the optician afterwards, they had been purposefully selected for this task – as if all their lives they'd been subconsciously practising for this day.

As well as Gabriele's radio call, he knew the girls had telephoned the emergency services from Elena's mobile, but there was no sign of backup. Now it was fully light and the optician could make out dots over a 500-metre radius.

'Propeller!' he screamed. 'We need to go slower! We're going to slice them up with the bloody propeller!'

Galata zigzagged through the small waves, picking her way through the debris of corpses and discarded clothing and shoes. It felt so ugly, thought the optician, not to stop and retrieve the dead, but they could not matter now. Not while there were others out there who still had life in them, who still had a chance.

They were so close to the end – the next two men they dragged from the sea – that the optician feared they'd die on board. Salt water and shock had wrecked their intestines and they were retching and defecating all over the deck. Their eyelids fluttered as they drifted in and out of consciousness. Their bodies were exhausted with the struggle and their spirits were only just flickering. Teresa and Maria tucked sleeping bags from the bunks around their shuddering forms, willing them to stay alive.

'Thirty metres away – 7 o'clock!' yelled Francesco.

There were four men in the next huddle, all clinging to each other, splayed out in an ungainly formation, splashing the water like dogs with their forearms as they tried to stay afloat. In the clear water, the soles of their feet flashed pink as they kicked upwards, thrashing like fish in a net. Kneeling with his arm outstretched, the optician waited for the fists to close on his.

He would never forget the feel of all those slippery wet hands in his. The power ripped through his own sinewy back as he willed survivors from the water. He had never felt so alive in his whole life – he could feel vitality sparking, flaring, flashing through his nerves and muscles and he wanted – no, he needed – to make those dots in the water feel it too. He felt he had the energy to reanimate them all if only he could reach them in time. His friends' zeal was electrifying and spurred him forward.

'Come on, guys, we need to move faster!'

One of the men they'd rescued was hysterical, jabbing his finger back down to the water, holding onto the optician and Francesco and pleading with Matteo who had pulled himself onto the stern's step. He kept repeating a word over and over again, but he didn't seem to understand any Italian.

It was Matteo who thought to try and speak in English. 'What do you want?' he urged him. 'We can help if you tell us slowly in English.'

The man looked at them all imploringly, tears pouring down his face 'Please,' he said, holding his hands together as if in prayer. 'Children. There are many children.'

Francesco had jumped in the water then too, kicking downwards, his eyes stinging in the salt water. He'd exploded back onto the surface of the water after a minute or so and had raced back to the boat like a man chased by a shark. The optician did not need an explanation and nor did any of the others – they all knew from the shock on Francesco's face that under the waves he'd been nudged and bumped by the blunt, clumsy forms of corpses.

The optician found himself praying silently to a God he didn't believe in. Just save the children. Please let us find the children. Whatever happens, for God's sake let me help the children.

But they never found any children.

'Let's move on!' said Francesco determinedly and Gabriele thrust the engine forward.

By the time they reached the trio of people Maria had spotted, there were only two heads left above the water level.

'It's a woman!' Maria leant over the side of the boat as Gabriele steered it tentatively towards the group. 'There's a man too, but I'm sure there's a woman!'

Francesco threw the rubber ring to the woman, but it was the man who caught it. The optician watched as the man pulled it towards her but she seemed disinterested and wouldn't grab it despite his frantic cajoling. Her left hand lay across the bobbing back of the dead man beside her and her head, with its long braids splayed out like tentacles in the water, drooped sideways; it was clear she was giving up and was going the same way as the corpse she clung to. The man in the water beside her tried to prise her hands and place them on the ring, clearly pleading with her to let the dead man go.

The optician knew it was futile to plead in Italian, but he did it all the same. Teresa and Maria cried out to her to stay with them, reassuring her that it would soon all be over. At the sound of the female voices, the young woman opened her eyes, raised her chin slightly and looked at them. Squeezing the last drop of her strength, she lifted her arm and flopped it onto the ring. She was wearing a turquoise T-shirt that was slicked with oil – and nothing else.

It was almost as if she hadn't wanted to be saved, the

optician thought; she was so reluctant to leave the lifeless form beside her. She slithered onto the deck in a pool of diesel and seawater like a landed fish with the struggle gone out of it. When he put his hand to her cheek, she cowered, her hands pulling down at the hem of her T-shirt, trying to hide her nudity and humiliation. He wanted desperately to reassure her, but her fear of him, of Francesco and Matteo, was tangible; he could feel they were hurting her just by looking at her.

Yet when Teresa laid a beach towel over her body, she sat up instantly and touched Teresa's hand. 'Thank you,' she whispered in English in a cracked voice and wrapped the towel around her waist. As they tried to comfort this slightly built woman, Teresa and Maria were weeping openly, but the young woman remained impassive. She sat with her chin slightly upwards, looking, thought the optician, almost haughty as she choked back her grief. Was she too proud to weep or just too broken? In their own patchy English and with much sign language, they showered her with questions: did she want water, did she want to take off the wet turquoise T-shirt and put on the dry sweatshirt they were proffering, was the dead man she had clung to her husband and were there any other women on board?

She had responded only to the last question. She turned her head to the sea again where the corpse was still visible, floating crudely, face downwards in the swell. She stared at the form for a long moment before shuffling round on her bottom and turning her back. 'He was my brother,' she said quietly and without self-pity. 'And yes, we were many women.'

She did not speak again, and although they all checked on her frequently, none of them once saw her cry. Nor did they find any other women.

Chapter 5

Everywhere he looked, there were more of them! They seemed to multiply in the water, hands breeding hands. The optician looked at his watch and felt panic rise up in his throat – he knew they were working against the clock here. Where the hell was the coastguard? All this time he was being taunted by the nagging doubt that they weren't doing this right, that a professional crew would be doing things differently, more efficiently, and would be saving more people. If only they could work faster!

The women had ransacked the boat: when they'd exhausted all the clothes from everyone's bags and rucksacks, they'd torn down the curtains from the cabin windows; even the rough fabric of the banquettes had been unzipped and yanked off to try to give the survivors some dignity. Some men had been so mortified to see women aboard and to have to stand before them naked that they'd tried to hurl themselves back into the water.

They'd thrown the lifebuoy to a solitary man whom the optician had spotted waving to them frantically, but they'd all agreed stoically they had to plough on towards a group of five people some 50 metres away who were clawing and clutching at each other's bodies. He had tried to keep eye contact with the man while they were rescuing the others, calling out to him constantly, promising him they were coming back for him, that he would be saved. But by the time they'd returned, the man had peeled away from the ring and the sea had taken him. No one had spoken when the optician fished the empty lifebuoy back on board. It had felt mockingly light.

Two fishing boats, responding to the pan-pan call, arrived shortly afterwards. Gabriele had sounded the horn and *Galata's* crew and the rescued migrants had all yelled at the skippers to slow down because they were afraid the propellers would shred the people still in the water. The optician saw the fishing boats hesitate – from that distance they'd only have seen a boatload of black people – as there were of course strict laws about aiding illegal immigrants and they were afraid to intervene. He felt the fury surge up in him again. How could it be possible that Italy put the law above human lives? He looked at the jumble of wretched survivors crouched on the deck, partially draped in seat covers, in his own old T-shirts and shorts, sobbing for their dead, for their lost women and children. The deck was awash with their vomit, tears and faeces.

He was tired now, but he mustn't admit it. He'd almost slipped off the stern step himself during the last rescue; it had felt like his arms were stuffed with cotton wool rather than muscles and sinews when he'd tugged the writhing body on board and thumped it down onto the deck. His legs were quivering. But he had to ignore his body's complaints. He had to keep rescuing them. There were still people in the water and they needed him.

He had no idea how many they'd saved now, but the boat was bloated. The stern step was almost level with the waterline; it was clear they were too low in the water. *Galata* was becoming capricious under the strain and was no longer responding obediently to Gabriele's commands. Her buoyancy compromised, she was becoming sluggish and dangerously out of control. But there were still more people in the water.

Off portside, they could see one of the fishing boats had begun to pluck the corpses that were littered across the sea. Bodies, swollen with seawater, were slapped down rudely and heavily one by one like cuts of meat. Somebody's wife, somebody's brother, somebody's son.

The optician clambered back up onto the cabin roof to his original viewpoint and began furiously scouring the sea for anything giving off a sign of life. He needed to feel the grasp of another hand, needed to feel fingers lock into his, bone grinding on bone. He was shaking with nervous energy.

'There! Two people! At three o clock!'

Galata cut drunkenly and unsteadily through the little waves as Gabriele forced the little boat to turn against her will. Her fenders smacked and bounced across the surface, kicking up spray as the optician scrambled down onto the deck. Matteo was already on his stomach, hanging over the step ready to throw the rubber ring to the thrashing hands. Come on! Come on! The heads were going under; only the hands, now clenched into fists, were visible. Don't you die! Don't you dare die!

They tore those men from the water. They grabbed at the fists and yanked the hair on the submerged heads until the faces of the drowning men, eyes rolling with pain, emerged, shocked, above the surface. The optician felt fingers solder onto his. Francesco and Matteo almost tossed the first spluttering man on board; he felt the same untamed energy race through his own veins and he roared as Matteo helped him pitch the second man onto the deck.

Gabriele was shouting now from the wheelhouse that he could no longer control the boat. The optician could feel her straining under the weight of them as she slipped lower in the water. Without warning, panic flooded his stomach. How long could *Galata* hold them up? He looked at Teresa stroking a man's forehead as he tried to sip water from a bottle, her small frame supporting the weight of his lolling neck. The boys would never forgive him if he put their mother's life in danger. They would never ever forgive him. But there were still people in the water!

The two short blasts from the coastguard's horn came just as Gabriele was yelling that they needed to start chucking water and stuff from the cabin overboard to lighten the load. At the sound of the horn, the survivors moved as a single herd starboard and, unnerved by the sudden movement, the boat began to tilt and loll, tilt and loll. The migrants began to scream in panic.

'Get back! Get back over here! Quickly!' screamed the optician.

Back up on the cabin roof, the optician had fallen on his knees and was clinging to the little barrier with his right arm while waving frantically at the men with his left, screaming at them to move back. Matteo and Francesco were losing their footing as the boat swayed violently; they were shouting and pushing the men to the other side of the boat.

'Move! We'll tip over! Move!'

Galata shuddered dangerously before sagging back into the water, belching with her overload.

Shaking, the optician got to his feet again and watched the red and white coastguard ship approach, with its orange zodiac alongside. He had no idea how many people were on board *Galata* now, but he knew it was too many. From his vantage point he did a rapid head count. One, two, twenty . . . forty-six men and one woman. Plus eight crew. That meant there were fifty-five of them. Fifty-five on a boat built for a maximum of ten.

Underneath him he could hear the crackles of the VHF radio as Gabriele talked to the approaching coastguard. He felt relief that the professionals were coming, that they would soon transfer the migrants they'd rescued to the coastguard's boat so that *Galata* could continue the search for survivors without putting anyone's life at risk. Come on, come on! They'd be even more efficient now with the professional teams here telling them what to do. It would be good to follow orders: under their tutelage, they'd save more people, more quickly. The men on the deck were looking up at him expectantly. It would be OK. They'd find these survivors' friends and their families. They'd do it.

He glanced down at his wife. It might be best, though, if Teresa went with the migrants on the coastguard's boat; she'd been so tough out here. Really, she'd been incredible looking out for everyone, thinking on her feet, never stopping for a second. But obviously they, the men, they had to carry on with the search. They had to.

He heard Gabriele raise his voice. Gabriele was shouting from the wheelhouse across to the coastguard ship that was now alongside *Galata*'s hull.

'No! You have to take them! We need to keep looking – there are still people in the water!'

The optician squinted down and saw a coastguard officer repeatedly crossing and uncrossing his wrists in a gesture that clearly meant, 'Finish'. Surely the officer wasn't telling them they had to give up the search? No, he couldn't be. It would be unthinkable to stop. It would be madness! Was that a hand just there, under the lip of that curled wave or just a shadow? Focus, man! Did something just move out there? His eyes probed the sea. Was there someone there? He blinked and tried to force his vision into focus as the big blue expanse stared back at him.

If it was a hand, it was gone now. The sea rolled over itself in front of him, its discreet waves unforthcoming. Had it been a hand? Had he missed it? His eyeballs throbbed with the effort of concentration. He had to stay focused.

Elena and Maria had joined in the now heated discussion

with the coastguard's captain and Matteo was arguing furiously. 'Just take some of the passengers! We can carry on here! Don't be ridiculous!'

Francesco was swearing.

The optician felt his heart pounding. They were being told to abandon the search. They were really being told to give up. It was crazy! This was pure madness – they couldn't give up . . . They couldn't give up on these people now. They'd saved forty-seven people, damn it! They just needed some help to offload the survivors. For pity's sake, it was unthinkable to put the brakes on the rescue, to give up on these poor people who were counting on them to find the others. Come on!

'Hey!' he shouted down to the coastguard aggressively. 'There are women and children in the water. We've got to find them and we're wasting time. For God's sake, we don't have time!'

The captain stood firm. It was too dangerous, he insisted, to attempt a transfer of passengers at sea and anyway, protocol forbade such a move. What they were proposing was against official procedure because it could further endanger lives. It was also clear, insisted the captain, that *Galata*'s crew was exhausted after hours of searching and needed to stop. So the coastguard, he continued coolly, would take *Galata*'s place as the search and rescue mission alongside the fishing boats. *Galata* must return to Lampedusa's port immediately with the migrant survivors who would be taken to the reception centre for medical attention. He crossed his arms to make an X-shape. Other boats were now on hand and the time had come to stop.

It was over.

An officer on the coastguard ship took a photograph of *Galata* that day at the moment that the captain was giving his orders. She'd sunk so low in the water that one of her fenders was half-submerged and a young man sitting in the optician's apple-green swimming shorts, with his legs dangling through the safety rail, lets his feet drag on the surface. The picture's a little blurry, but you can make out Gabriele leaning out of the wheelhouse, his high forehead wrinkled as he strains to hear what's being said by the coastguard, while a migrant man, perhaps the man most freshly plucked from the sea, peeps out from behind a white bedsheet.

On the roof of the wheelhouse, the optician, wearing rolled-up royal blue trousers, has his strong bare back to the camera. He's caught in mid-spin, standing with his weight on his right leg, his left leg about to swing round. His gaze is fixed firmly ahead on the huge expanse of water before him and his left arm is poised as if he's about to shout: 'There! Two hands at nine o'clock!'

You can see very clearly that it isn't over for the optician. He's still searching, still scouring and still desperate to save lives.

Chapter 6

They cut a pathetic sight as they headed slowly back to port, *Galata* moving sulkily through the water, groaning under her heavy load and protesting each time the sea, bullied a little by the rising wind, made her path choppier and more difficult. Inside she had been ravaged: her curtains torn, her cabin shredded; outside, her deck was covered in filth, her motley, ragged crew slumped against her gunwale in abject grief. Almost everyone was crying. The original shrieks of terror had been replaced by a doleful sobbing that made the optician's heart ache.

At the bow, sitting apart, was the only woman they had managed to rescue, her eyes fixed firmly on the approaching land, on the shores of Europe that the optician imagined she must have waited for with such hope. Her grief was impenetrable; way deeper, he suspected as he scanned her face, than the open sea where her brother and compatriots had just sunk to their deaths. Her suffering seemed so vast and intensely private that he felt almost fearful as he watched her.

Almost no one spoke. Teresa, weeping with the men, held their hands and patted shoulders, offering water and biscuits silently, mothering and comforting. He knew he should go to her, to take her hand in his, but he dare not trust himself to stay strong in her embrace. Of course he was exhausted now; he could feel his body was running on empty. But more than his physical fatigue, he felt acutely that something fundamental inside him had fractured and had splintered away. Something had gone from him, had been lifted out of him and lost.

He looked down towards the glittering water. He'd always respected the sea, had always known it was far bigger and more powerful than him; yet he always felt a sense of kinship whenever he looked out at its sparkling surface. Now he sensed its hostility – or at least its ambiguity – knowing how stealthily and purposefully it had sucked down so many lives into its depths. How many more migrant boats were secretly beached on its bottom? How many more desperate people had given their last breath to its mighty waves? He cast an eye over the men they'd rescued, the men who had cheated the sea. At just 15 metres long, *Galata* barely registered on its enormous expanse. The sea was just teasing them, just letting them think they'd won. In the rippling backwash, he could almost hear it laughing, taunting him about those he'd left behind in its grasp.

They had to go back. They had to! They would drop the survivors at the port and they'd turn around again. He felt the familiar nervous energy trickle back through his veins. Of course Gabriele would agree. And he could always count on Francesco and Matteo. They'd go back.

The optician was shocked by the numbers of police and officials in uniform at the port. They swarmed all over the quayside, radioing, pacing up and down and crowding out curious bystanders. As they docked, some of the migrants cowered back at the sight of their guns and truncheons and the harsh sound of the sirens of the police vans. He found himself angry again, wanting to warn them to back off, and he saw similar feelings in his friends' faces. For God's sake, stop treating them like criminals! You have no damn idea what these people have just been through! Teresa had pushed forward to *Galata*'s bow, protecting her charges with her own body like an animal might do.

She had gone to pieces when the men were helped off the boat and put in the police vans. She had crumpled onto her knees on the quayside and howled like a mother being separated from her children. They'd prised her away from the first man they'd rescued – the teenager to whom she had given her vermilion coloured T-shirt. She had clung to his hand with both of hers, and when the police officer separated them she had become hysterical with grief. Maria was the same – Francesco had sat down on the pavement with her until she'd stopped shaking. Elena and Giulia sobbed uncontrollably in each other's arms; they didn't look when the police vans started their engines. The optician wished he hadn't. He saw the frightened faces stare back at him through the windows, fingers pressed on the glass expectantly and he was overwhelmed with a sense of guilt that he hadn't saved more.

He felt helpless. He had no common language with which he could reassure these desperate people, and even if he had, he thought bitterly, what could he tell them? That it would be OK and that they would all live happily ever after? He had no idea what the procedure was, he had no clue what was about to happen to them now.

'Some of them are very ill!' he shouted through the open window of the police van. 'They need medical help! Please – they've been in the water for hours.'

The officer gave him the thumbs-up sign and his electric window slid silently shut. The van pulled away.

Matteo and Gabriele were back on the boat, already sluicing down the fouled deck with the hose. Francesco was talking to a police officer, giving him an official statement of what had happened. As he approached them, he heard Francesco say that the sea was 'thick with bodies'. He interrupted politely and asked the officer if they could give their statements a little later, perhaps that afternoon or in the evening. They'd like, he explained, to rejoin the rescue operation.

The policeman, a heavy man with a weather-worn face looked at him, puzzled.

'Mate,' he said not unkindly. 'We've got six boats out there looking now. But it's been hours. This isn't a rescue mission any more – it's a recovery operation. We've just called in the diving squad.'

So it really was over.

The women walked home slowly together – the optician and the other men stayed to clean *Galata*. They worked quietly and efficiently, saying little to one another as they scrubbed the salty stains from the boat's keel, tidied away ropes and bagged rubbish. The optician had the impression they were all overly deliberate with their tasks – none of them seemed in any hurry to call it a day. When they'd eventually parted, though, at the foot of the little hill leading to the town, they'd hugged each other fiercely, like brothers.

Teresa was still sobbing when he came in. She told him she couldn't stop, she didn't know how to stop. He held her in his arms and felt her slim, fragile body shudder against his, but found that he just didn't know what to say, he didn't how to comfort her. He couldn't even make sense of the day's narrative himself; he could find no interpretation of the events that would soften the impact for her.

As he cuddled his wife close to him, he could still feel the cold, oily skin of that first young man they had plucked from the water – he remembered the boy's heart thumping against his own bare chest, remembered his own visceral joy at feeling the very life in him.

He cried a little in the shower. It felt wrong to be comforting himself under this hot water, to be washing clean away the sweat and tears and grease of this terrible day. He kept thinking of the children they were supposed to find but hadn't, kept thinking how frightened they must have been as the seawater had started to pour into their boat. Mustn't. Mustn't think of that, mustn't let himself think of that. But what if there were still people out there, people who were lost and overlooked by the fishing boats and the coastguard? What if they were waiting for him?

He had always been a man who had been pretty confident about where he was going, pretty sure of himself and his decisions. Now he felt that same unnerving splintered feeling he'd sensed on the sad journey back to port. It was as if he'd left a part of himself back in the waves with those he had not been able to save.

Had he given all he could? His brain started racing, his memory bringing to the surface vague and filmy layers of detail about all the other shipwrecks he knew had already occurred off Lampedusa's coast. He remembered switching off the radio last week when they'd talked about migrants drowning off the coast of Sicily. He had turned away from them.

He lifted his face to the showerhead and let the water drum over his closed eyes and mouth. His father had always told him that in each of us there is a thick black line above and below which we can measure ourselves and our behaviour and against which we can evaluate what is right and what is wrong. He had always felt that black line strongly in himself and had calculated his actions, his priorities and his values accordingly against it. He knew when he'd fallen below the mark and his internal meter warned him when he was about to make a mistake. He checked his life against that bar. And now the line didn't seem straight or constant any more. It was wavy and intermittent and he could no longer see his position in relation to it. The certainty was gone. He let the hot water pound down onto his throat and chest, but found no solace in it.

He went to work that afternoon. Immersing himself in work, in the usual routines, that was the only way that he might hope to get his thoughts tidied and filed away again neatly, to glue back together his fragmented sense of order. Teresa had passed out with nervous exhaustion on the bed and he'd found something to eat in the fridge and had gone downstairs to open the shop. He spent a couple of hours going over his stock lists, called a supplier in Naples and repaired a pair of sunglasses for a couple of elderly German tourists who had come to the island.

He behaved professionally, smiled politely, yet all the time he had a scathing sense of how absurd it all was. The pathetic unimportance of his routines and the insignificance of his work compared with this morning when he had really known he was alive! This morning had actually mattered.

Unconsciously, he let his hands ball into fists and the aching muscles in his arms tensed, ready to take the strain. He saw the yellowing eyes full of terror, the shivering naked bodies slicked with the slime of diesel oil, the trembling forms cowering under gaudy beach towels. He realized that he was aching to be back with them. He wanted to take their hands again, to talk to them. He wanted to sit down with them, to ask how they were, who they were, why they'd come here. He wanted to know if the fishing boats or the coastguards had found their families, if they'd been reunited with their loved ones. He had to know what happened. He would not give up on them.

Quickly he shut and locked the shop and ran up the stairs to the apartment. Teresa jumped as he pushed open the door and he saw she had her mobile in her hand and that her face was still raw from crying.

'I was speaking to Giulia,' she told him tearfully, lifting her phone. 'And we're all agreed. We want to go to the reception centre this evening. We need to see them.'

Chapter 7

It was only a ten or fifteen-minute stroll to the reception centre; they hadn't needed the scooter. The lay-bys and verges on the slip road leading up to the place were jam-packed with parked police cars and vans, all crammed in as tightly and skilfully, the optician remarked to Gabriele, as the football fans' cars outside the San Paolo stadium when Napoli were playing at home. They had to step out into the road to avoid the jutting bumpers.

An elderly couple, hand in hand and both dressed in red fleeces, were walking unsteadily towards them. The optician winced involuntarily as he saw the man's cheap navy trousers flapping above his anklebone; they were a good three or four centimetres shy of an acceptable length.

'Good evening!'

The couple smiled widely as they approached and then, clearly recognizing Francesco from somewhere, stopped to exchange some pleasantries with him, asking how he was, how his daughter's ice-cream parlour was doing. They always bought their ice cream from her, you know, the man assured Francesco, because she was the best in Lampedusa. The optician caught the woman smiling distinctly at him as if they knew each other too, but he couldn't quite place her. He was sure he had not fitted her with glasses in the last couple of years. He prided himself on having an excellent memory for his customer's faces. He half smiled back, uncertain.

The elderly man jabbed his thumb over his shoulder in the direction of the reception centre gates and said, wasn't it a terrible business that had happened today with that shipwreck? Police reckoned hundreds had been lost. His voice cracked a little as he talked and his wife patted his arm reassuringly. They'd just come up to deliver some second-hand clothes, he explained, for the survivors. Poor buggers had been left with nothing.

Briefly, Francesco outlined for them what had happened that morning on board *Galata*. How they had seen all those people in the sea and how they had tried to save as many as they could. He gave few details. While Francesco told their tale, the optician scuffed the toe of his trainer on the ground and watched the patterns he made in the dirt.

They were so shocked, the old couple. The lady whimpered, her hands in front of her mouth while fat tears rolled into the deep crevices of her cheeks. The old chap was crying too, crossing himself and looking up to the heavens, perhaps to thank God for sending *Galata* to the migrants or perhaps, thought the optician wryly, to ask why the hell He had let the tragedy happen in the first place. So brave, the old lady was saying to them. You are all so brave.

He didn't look up.

He heard the elderly couple make their excuses and wish everyone a good evening. He lifted his gaze and met the eyes of the old lady, whose head was slightly sloped to one side, studying him. She smiled sympathetically, leaned forward then, and squeezed his arm hard. 'God bless, dear,' she said and limped off, her hand searching for her husband's.

He remembered who she was then. She was the woman who'd come to the shop the other day looking for cast-off clothing and shoes. The woman he had turned away.

He flinched as a large mottled-brown dog slinked past his right thigh, its thin rat-like tail curling high over its back. It hurried towards the heavy wire gates of the reception centre, pawing and rubbing its mangy head on the mesh, trying to attract the guard's attention. The optician watched a young officer grin as he got up to open the door.

'Cheeky monkey!' he quipped, aiming a pretend kick at the dog's hindquarters. 'You just can't get enough of these guys, can you?'

Ignoring his protector, the dog made a beeline for the supper queue, trotting towards a group of migrant men who the optician could see were squatting in the dust, rough army blankets over their shoulders, spooning something from plastic pots. The dog sat down in front of them and licked its black lips expectantly.

As the optician and his friends approached the gates, the metal doors clanged shut.

'Hey! Wait a minute!' shouted the optician. 'Can you let us in, please? We are looking for . . . we are looking for the people who arrived here this morning.'

The guard looked at them sceptically. 'Which NGO are you from, then?' he asked, chewing gum as he studied their faces and searched the optician's chest for an ID badge.

'No, no,' said the optician impatiently, dismissing the idea with his hand. 'We're not from any organization. It's just that we . . . we know some of the people who arrived this morning and we need to see them.'

Teresa stepped forward. 'We really need to see them urgently,' she insisted. 'It's very important.'

The guard chewed for a while, then shrugged. 'Members of the public can't come into the reception centre,' he said firmly. He drew his head back and shot them a quizzical look. 'Are you journalists? Because if you are, you should know that the mayor has already given a statement on what happened this morning and you won't get any interviews with the migrants, OK?'

'We don't want interviews!' snapped the optician as the

others shifted irritably and began muttering protests. 'We need to talk to them, OK? Look, we know these people. We . . . we pulled them from the water this morning.'

'No can do, mate,' said the guard amiably. He took off his cap and swept his hair back from his forehead. 'But that was you guys, was it? Well! That was some rescue you pulled off – they reckon hundreds drowned out there today.'

He retreated back to his little sentry box, calling over his shoulder that he'd radio the chief to see what he could do.

The optician and Maria put their fingers through the wire fence and peered through at the group of migrants they could make out in the dusky light eating by the trees. Were they the people they'd saved today? Was it they who had sat weeping on the deck of their boat, gasping the sweet air of life? Teresa and Giulia waved tentatively at the group, but the men, intent on eating, seemed to stare through them and no one waved back. As they finished their rations, the inmates casually chucked their plastic pots on the ground and the dog was quick to take his chance, snatching them one by one and dragging them a little way off to the treeline to enjoy alone.

Squinting through the fence like this, it was difficult to make out what the reception centre was comprised of. On the right-hand side there seemed only to be heavy trees and on the left there were a series of low, nondescript whitewashed buildings that were so uniform and anonymous they might equally be offices or dormitories. In front of the far buildings, scores of police in dark blue uniforms patrolled.

'Chief's busy!' shouted the guard leaning out of his sentry box. 'But the answer's no!' He stepped back inside his sentry box and picked up the phone.

'Hey!' the optician yelled back. 'Don't turn your back on us! Get someone else to come and talk to us – we need to get in!' He rattled the fence. 'Hey!'

The guard quietly shut his door.

Steep grassy banks flanked the right-hand side of the path outside the reception centre and they were thick with litter. Matteo tried scrambling up, but slid back down, his foot skidding on a half-empty pizza box. He cursed and wiped the tomato sauce from his shoe on the coarse foliage before trying again, a little further away from the gates. This time he successfully clambered up onto the ridge. He called to the others.

'Come on! Up here we can walk along the side fence and we might be able to see into those buildings.'

Small stones cascaded from the face of the dry bank as they climbed up one after the other. The optician held out his hand to steady Elena, who was slipping in her sandals; his heart bounced in his chest as her fingers gripped his.

There was a jumble of discarded clothing on the ridge. A couple of playing cards buckled in the evening breeze, imprisoned in the spikes of tough grass, and a small black notebook, swollen and crimped from having been waterlogged, fanned its drying pages. Francesco picked it up and leafed through it, but its content had run off the pages. Gabriele drew their attention to a bright red sweatshirt proclaiming the improbable slogan 'Welcome to California!' and underneath it, when Teresa kicked it aside, they saw a tiny, faded green and white baby-grow with holes in the toes.

They walked on gingerly. The optician felt something rubbery under his trainer and he jumped back with a gasp. He lifted his foot and saw that he'd trodden on the head of a limbless plastic doll whose contorted face, tattooed now with the imprint of his shoe sole, stared up at the sky with a single sea-blue eye. Her left eye had been pushed deep into its socket by the weight of his foot and a battery in her chest cavity bled a rusty liquid onto the patchy grass. There was something deeply disturbing about the battered doll. He lagged behind for a couple of seconds and then, with the top of his foot, scooped up a dirty pair of shorts and covered the doll's nakedness with them.

The mangy dog started barking furiously the moment they got to the fence, fearing, the optician imagined, competition for his pasta pots. He raced up at the bank and snarled through the mesh at them, his ragged beard crusty with tomato sauce. The men whom they'd watched eating stopped chatting together and looked up blankly. Maria called down to them in English and a couple of the men raised a hand suspiciously in greeting. They showed no recognition of *Galata*'s crew. It couldn't be them.

They edged further along the perimeter fence and the dog followed them, growling his displeasure. Standing under a huge carport structure, hundreds of black men in jogging pants and flip-flops sat slumped dejectedly on concrete benches or leaned against the pillars, yawning. The optician looked hard at them, trying to recognize faces. Maria yelled out again to the men, setting the dog into a frenzied rage. One of the men stirred, glanced up and then peeled himself from a bench and began to amble his way towards them, slowly scaling the prickly bank in his flip-flops.

'Very sad day,' he said in halting Italian. 'Many of my countrymen dies and everyone here is crying. You journalists, yes?' They all began to talk over one another in their haste to clarify why they had come. The man clasped his hands together. 'God bless you,' he said, drawing a small coloured wooden crucifix from his pocket. 'Here there are many good people who help us. And all we Eritreans say thank you.' He kissed the cross. 'You were not the first boat to reach them, you know,' he sighed. 'Another boat passed them but it did not stop.'

An exclamation of protest rippled through *Galata*'s crew.

The optician clutched the man's T-shirt through the fence. 'That's not possible!' he cried out. 'That can't be true. Who wouldn't stop when they saw people in trouble?'

They were all pressed close against the fence now.

'No!' protested Gabriele. 'No no, no!' His skin had a waxy look to it. The Eritrean shook his head sadly and was just beginning to speak again when a policeman, alerted by the commotion caused by the dog, blew his whistle sharply. The man hastily scarpered back down the bank to take up his former place on the concrete bench and stared again at the ground.

The policeman clapped his hands. 'Get down from there!' he warned. 'You're not allowed up there!' It was clear that he wasn't talking to the dog.

A few of his colleagues joined him curiously and the optician shouted back down to them, explaining what they were doing and why they were there. His fingers, locked around the mesh of the fence, were white and he'd pressed his forehead against the plastic green wire.

'I don't care who you are,' retorted one of the police officers. 'You can't come in here and you can't talk to the illegal immigrants.'

The women protested, pleading with the guards to just give them some news about the people they'd rescued. But the guards, shaking their heads very deliberately, were not backing down. Matteo kicked the fence in frustration. The optician understood the gesture. It felt like they'd lost them all over again.

'Oh, please,' cried Teresa coming forward too and holding the fence. 'Please just let us see them for five minutes. Just five minutes!' She looked at her husband imploringly.

' It's very important for us,' he tried, his voice breaking a little. 'They're our . . . they're my . . .' He stopped abruptly.

What were they to him? They could not be described as friends; he did not even know their names or where they came from. Yet he felt a bond with them that went way beyond a friendship. The people he had rescued were on the brink of existence. And when he had held their hands in his, when he had watched them take their first breaths on *Galata*'s deck, he knew he had touched the very essence of life. They had looked him in the eye and they had chosen to live.

And yet another boat had apparently chosen to leave them in the water, had sailed past them, shrugging them off, blinking them out of sight. He felt winded by what the Eritrean had told them and he could see his own shock reflected in Francesco's face, in Elena's, in Gabriele's. Did he know them, these people who had not stopped? Did he perhaps eat in their restaurants, shake their hands, did he advise them on choosing the right glasses for their face shape?

He was reminded of a dinner he had once had in Naples with his father when he was a young man, on the cusp of adulthood. It had just been the two of them and his father had spoken to him man to man about how the war had left him disillusioned with human nature. All of us, his father had warned, carry a latent tendency to cruelty and indifference in our hearts; we are all capable of terrible things. But his father's words had seemed irrelevant to his own comfortable post-war generation. Of course the young optician had seen the images of emaciated bodies festering in putrid concentration camps, but they seemed to have nothing to do with the people he knew and mixed with. He remembered telling his father confidently that such horror was locked safely in the past, that lessons had been learnt, and he remembered too his father's fond and sad smile. He saw again those thin, naked bodies lying on *Galata*'s deck and the shocked, staring eyes.

Teresa gently uncurled his fingers from the wire.

He shrank back from the main gates when he saw a couple of camera crews had arrived and were trying to film the inhabitants through the mesh. A small group of journalists were arguing heatedly through the gate with a couple of guards. Giulia approached one of the women she knew from the local paper, pressing her for details about what had happened with the fishing boat and coastguard. She hurried back to the others.

'They saved about a hundred more!' she exclaimed. 'They are all from Eritrea and Somalia. And they found the children!'

One of the male journalists wearing a smart black jacket turned around from the fence as he overheard her conversation. He looked cocky, thought the optician, a know-it-all.

'They found the children dead,' the journalist corrected Giulia. 'Most of the women and children were below deck so they all drowned. They were mainly from Eritrea, with a few Somalis, I think.' He flicked through his writing pad, checking through some scribbled notes and said coolly: 'And it looks like their boat went down around two this morning, so half of those who got out would have copped it anyway in the water.' The journalist raised his eyebrows. 'The migrants have told the police that a boat went past them without stopping. Bound to be an investigation there.' He turned over another page. 'Police confirm the first boat that started rescuing them didn't spot them till gone six apparently.'

The optician caught his sleeve and asked him to clarify the timings of the shipwreck. An ugly image floated to the front of his mind. He saw himself lying on his bunk on board *Galata* that morning, grinning smugly about being on holiday and debating whether he could be bothered to make coffee as he lay on his back listening to the seagulls screeching. Listening to the people screeching. Listening to the drowning desperate people begging for help. People who had been in the water for four hours already.

'Are you locals?' asked the journalist hopefully. 'Because apparently it was a group of islanders who were first on the scene and I heard they saved about forty migrants from drowning.'

It was Giulia's turn to contradict. 'It was forty-seven,' she said firmly. 'I know because it was us on that boat.'

They were surrounded immediately. Cameras began snapping at their faces; reporters quarrelled with one another as they shouldered their way to the front of the scrum. Francesco and Matteo looked bewildered as the man in the black jacket swiftly fixed tiny microphones onto the lapels of their shirts, tucking the wires into their trouser pockets. Questions were fired at them one after another.

'How did you know there was a shipwreck?'

'How did you feel when you first realized what was happening?'

'How did you manage to rescue all those people?

'How do you feel about the migration problem in Italy?'

Surreptitiously the optician edged back from the crowd, pulling Teresa with him. They were both too shy for all this publicity and he was not going to have his sensitive wife subjected to a grilling by these people. He could hear the emotion in his friends' voices as they tried to recount the details of the terrible day into the various microphones. Maria was wavering a little, her staccato account punctuated by deep breaths and several sweeps of her hand across her eyes. The questions were incessant.

The optician turned and looked behind him into the reception centre. The mottled brown dog, sated now with food, had stolen a sock from one of the migrants and was tossing it in the air and chasing it like an oversized puppy, rolling contentedly on his back in the dust. Somewhere in there, in one of those white buildings, were the forty-seven people they had pulled from the water. And that bloody stray dog was free to bother and pester them, whereas he was being told he had no right to even ask how they were!

On the far side of the path a gentle-looking man of about his own age seemed deep in conversation with a young African man in a Manchester United football shirt. The African's head was dropped low on his shoulders as the older man gently steered him towards the gate and pressed the intercom. When the guard got up to open the gate, the man placed a fatherly hand on the young man's arm and handed him what looked like a little wooden crucifix on a string. Like the one, realized the optician, that the Eritrean man they had just met on the ridge had shown them. The centre's gates opened and he watched the man hug the young asylum-seeker to him. The guard waited patiently, showing no sign of irritation, and the African sloped off towards the white buildings. Before shutting the gate again, the guard chatted amicably with the man who had given the little cross to the young migrant and shook his hand warmly. The optician could not hear all their conversation, but he caught enough of the Lampedusan dialect to know they were both local. It was clear the man was a regular here.

The optician wondered why he had never visited the reception centre until now.

He could hear many more cars pulling up in the lane, and the journalists who were still recording flinched as the beeping of locking systems and the slamming of car doors cut rudely across their interviews. They must be double-parked down there, thought the optician. There's so many of them they must be blocking one another in, parked back to back. What on earth are they all needed for, these officials and policemen, he wondered? What do they do? Well, whatever it was, he concluded, looking through the reception centre mesh at the migrants still huddled under their blankets, it clearly wasn't enough.

A brusque redhead from a national newspaper tapped him on the arm. She steered him further away from the media scrum and suggested they had a little talk. All she was really looking for, she explained, tossing back her red curls, was a really personal account of how it had felt to be on that boat, how it had felt to save everyone.

The optician looked at her blankly. 'But we didn't save everyone,' he responded flatly. The redhead acquiesced that of course he hadn't managed to save everyone, but even so, perhaps he could describe what she imagined must have been an exhilarating feeling when he had rescued people and perhaps what it was like to realize that some people were going to die before they could get to them.

'I mean, I'm guessing you had to play God out there, right?' she prompted him impatiently.

All those grasping hands. All those voices begging to be heard. And he had answered the prayers of just forty-seven of them. He searched her face. He could try to answer her questions, he could try to describe his feelings, but she would never really understand his answers. No one would ever understand, he thought, except for the seven others who were with him on board *Galata*. And they were all still trying to understand themselves what had happened. He declined the interview politely.

The local paper was clamouring for group photographs and individual headshots of each of them. The optician was as reluctant to have his picture taken as he was to answer questions, but he agreed to the photo. He blinked in the photographers' bright lights, his eyes always flitting towards the gates of the reception centre. Tomorrow, he thought, he would look up Eritrea on the computer.

The next morning he and Teresa were applauded as they walked into their usual café for coffee. The waiter flung the newspaper at him. There were photographs of the eight of them on the front page under the giant caption: 'Lampedusa's heroes', and a long article which commended their laudable courage.

He studied the pictures and saw eight faces haggard with exhaustion and grief. Francesco, the eldest among them, stared into the lens with an air of great responsibility as a father might do before he breaks terrible news to a child. Maria's face was so swollen with sorrow you wanted to reach out to try to soothe it with your fingertips. Matteo's eyes shone glassy and hostile with hurt.

In her photo, Teresa was half-smiling, looking at the lens with some bewilderment. She seemed to want to ask something; she seemed on the verge of summoning up the courage to beg someone to explain to her what had just happened. He felt his baldness made his own image look more exposed than the others. His mouth was twisted downwards on the right-hand side, and although he was looking directly at the camera through his well-chosen black-rimmed glasses, he looked utterly perplexed.

He folded over the paper angrily. I'm not a damned hero, he thought. I've failed. We've all failed. Us, Italy, Europe – all of us.

Chapter 8

It was too windy really; the palm trees were painfully contorted and a white plastic café chair that someone had forgotten to tie down was hurtling along the street on its back, but the optician had to go running all the same. He had to clear his head.

That morning in the shop, after he had returned from having his coffee, he had sat in front of the computer pretending to do paperwork, but instead had looked up every article he could find about Italy's former colony, Eritrea. The whole place, he'd learned, was run like a military garrison: every sixteen-year-old had to join the army and apparently the poor kids were stuck in it for life. The girls as well as the boys! He wasn't quite sure why he was being so secretive about what he was doing, but each time that he felt Teresa approaching, he had flipped the screen back onto his anodyne spreadsheets.

He'd read about the traffickers too, in the shop. He'd read the wretched testaments of migrants who'd fled through the Sahara and he had learned what the traffickers did to those desperate people who dared to dream of Europe. They stole their money and their mobile phones and beat them. As he tied his laces he remembered the proud-looking woman they had rescued yesterday, the woman in the turquoise T-shirt who had not cried. Did she have anyone to whom she could tell her story, someone who could comfort her? How was it possible that these people were so alone?

He picked up the photograph he kept on his desk and smiled

ruefully. It was a picture of his sons when they were adolescents, roaring with delight on a garish merry-go-round with their mother, radiant with joy at doing something so wonderfully childish, completely carefree. The optician closed the shop door behind him and winced at the buffeting wind. He thought of the faces on *Galata*'s deck. Some of those guys he'd pulled from the water had been so young – children really.

He hopscotched his way through the flying ice-cream pots and crisp packets that were freewheeling across the street. What family life, what kind of future could those kids have, he wondered, scattered all over their country in training camps, far away from home and forced to dig the fields or mend the roads? They were barely paid anything. He hadn't been able to finish the article about what happened to those who were caught absconding; reading about the brutality of Eritrea's prisons had made him nauseous.

Mind you, he snorted to himself as he ran past the sheltered terrace of a small café where a dozen or so *carabinieri* were installed sipping fruit juice, Lampedusa had started to look like a damned police state itself. Everywhere you went these days on the island, you were greeted with uniforms, truncheons and guns. It didn't exactly give an image of welcome.

A police siren began to wail in the distance and two squad cars came speeding over the little hill on the far side of the port, screeching to a dramatic halt as they veered onto the little track leading to the dock at Porto Favaloro. The optician knew they'd be waiting for the diving boats to come back from the wreck – he'd seen the coastguard's orange rubber dinghies hovering all day over the site of the sinking. Yesterday the fishing boats had apparently come back to port with their decks choked with bodies – how could there still be more out there?

But he had to see. He felt responsible. He knew some officious policeman or other would block him from walking directly onto the quayside at Porto Favaloro, so he jogged down onto the narrow strip of dirty sand and through the open flanks of the shipbuilding and metal yard which faced the quay. He could see the landing strip perfectly from there. Too perfectly.

The bodies were lined up across the concrete quay in plastic sheets the colour of green sludge, the same colour, he caught himself thinking, as the groundsheets he had used many years ago when he took his boys camping. Some were in long black body bags; others were zipped in white, like the sacks they used for recycling; a few were wrapped in surgical blue sheets. The bags bulged at the feet and here and there along the line the plastic was stretched into a pyramid form in the middle of the sack as if the hands were clasped together in prayer on the chest. A couple of the sacks were horribly baggy – children.

He wasn't ashamed of crying here. It seemed respectful to cry. He had little truck generally with the shenanigans of the Vatican, but this morning, on the radio, the Pope had been spot on when he'd said that today was a day for tears. A disgrace he'd called this tragedy. A disgrace we should all be ashamed of. He watched the coastguard divers swing another heavy dark sack onto the quayside. A big sack, then a medium sack and two little sacks.

He kept waiting for bags to move. He knew it was ridiculous, but it seemed impossible that these people didn't exist any more when their physical presence was still so apparent. He knew how their hands felt. He knew how their thin shoulder blades glinted when the sun threw down its light. He knew how they quivered with shame to be naked in front of women.

Why weren't they all laid the same way round? The first in the line had been placed with his head facing the sea; the next, packed tightly alongside, had his head facing the concrete steps of the dock with his feet towards the sea. Green, blue, black and white. It was a gruesome tessellation of death.

He smelt cigarette smoke and realized that he was no longer alone on the scrub of the beach. Lost in his thoughts, he had not heard the police diver's boots on the coarse sand. He greeted him and the diver nodded politely, his focus on the line of bodies laid out on the dock.

'Nearly 200 now,' he said and took a drag on his cigarette. 'I'm used to seeing horrors . . . but this? This is . . .' His face trembled as he fought back tears. 'I pulled out two little kids of maybe two and three years old from the cabin,' he told the optician. 'It was pitiful; they were wearing new shoes. Can you imagine? Their mum had bought them new patent leather shoes.' He nipped out his cigarette with his finger and thumb and immediately began to search his pockets for another.

The two men sat on the stumps of the breakwater with their chins supported in their hands and the optician confessed that he'd been out on the water yesterday, had been the first on the scene. He jerked his thumb towards the bodies. 'Weren't fast enough, were we?' he said bitterly. He had meant it as a rhetorical question, but the diver answered it anyway, explaining to the optician that those below deck would not have stood a chance. He seemed to anticipate the optician's next question.

'Don't know how long they'd have had,' he added. 'Not long . . . but enough time, I think, to understand what was coming. You see . . .' He hesitated for a long moment and let his foot tap against the wooden breakwater. 'You see, they were all holding hands.'

There had been a young woman, the diver said, dressed in a very white shirt and black trousers who was jammed against the cabin stairwell, blocking the door. When his buddy had yanked her arm to free her body, she had concertinaed and then sprung back, bringing with her a string of other bodies all joined at the hands. It was as if they'd become one giant singular entity, the diver said. Like a Christmas paper chain. There'd been a heavily pregnant woman at the back too. And mothers whose arms still encircled their little ones protectively, hugging them safe.

Who were they all? Did their families even know they'd left their homelands, let alone that they were dead? Even though his own boys were in their twenties now, Teresa always expected them to tell her if they were travelling anywhere and to clock in with her again when they'd arrived. And yet here were all these people, hundreds of them, anonymous in coloured sacks, known only as the woman in the white shirt and the toddler in the patent leather shoes.

'I'd better get back,' sighed the diver, getting up. 'The least we can do is bring them to shore.' He looked closely at the cigarette butt in his fingers for a moment and then held it up in the air, showing it to the optician. He smiled ironically. 'I gave this up five years ago,' he said.

Back on the road, the optician picked up the pace. He ran harder and faster than usual, forcing his body to cut through the wind. He could feel the shock of each footfall ricocheting through his vertebrae as his trainers pounded down on the tarmac. Wheezy little clouds of dust and fine sand blowing in from the coastal road made him cough and spit and his eyes smarted with grit.

The pity of those body bags! In life they had been robbed of a future and in death they'd been robbed of an identity.

He was inside the graveyard before he had made a conscious

decision to visit it. He'd been thinking about the body bags when suddenly there he was among the dense labyrinth of headstones, family vaults and mausoleums, all blanched by the strong sun.

They were beautifully kept, these graves; the gold and black lettering chiselled deep into the stone, small steel pots packed with dried flowers and weighted with bricks against the wind's caprices, standing guard at the foot of the tombs. Oval-shaped photographs glued to the marble prompted visitors to remember who the occupants had been. Here was eighty-two-year-old Rosa, smiling over a birthday cake; she'd been joined the following year by her husband Antonio, a retired doctor, pictured in a red sweater with a butterscotch-coloured cat in his arms. Andrea in the next plot had had a distinguished military career – in the 1940s wedding photograph with his wife Anna, his chest was already festooned with medals. Their son had joined them twenty years later. The optician brushed away the husk of a dried flower to read the inscription. He'd been a marine biologist apparently.

He walked the graveyard quietly, stopping every now and then when he spotted a name that registered with him or a headstone that intrigued him. He stooped to set upright a stainless steel pot of flowers that the wind had skittled. In the distance he could hear a tuneless whistling and the slow slapping sound of someone walking in flip-flops.

Halfway down the cemetery, he saw on his right a small unkempt patch of wasteland and he approached it curiously. The sandy earth was cracked dry and the fissures in the ground were choked with yellow dandelions and spiky sea grasses and gorses. A couple of flimsy wooden crosses, planted in a powdery block of cement, were trembling as they fought against the wind to stay rooted; many others had lost their battle and were lying face down in the thorn bushes. He turned one over with his foot and saw the number 8 had been inked on the join in faded black paint.

The slapping sound of the feet stopped beside him. An unshaven older man in a grey polo shirt flecked with white paint appeared and put down a spade and a pail of plaster.

'Poor buggers,' he said to the optician, chewing at his bottom lip with his one remaining tooth. 'I've worked in this graveyard for thirty years but I always nod to them when I pass.'

The optician looked at him blankly.

'The migrants,' the man explained matter-of-factly. 'The unknown migrants who've drowned off Lampedusa – I've buried them all. I'm the gravedigger here.' He began to pick at pieces of plaster that had lodged under his fingernails.

The optician looked down at the spade and felt himself recoil. A vision of the sludge-green body bags lined up on the quayside floated back into his mind. Is this where they were to end up? Dumped in a patch of weeds with a piece of unvarnished wood flung on top of them as an afterthought?

The gravedigger told him there were at least sixty migrant graves in the cemetery, squeezed in, he said, wherever they could find a space. Sometimes you could pop them on top of a long-gone family's vault; you couldn't do it with the tombs of those who still got visitors at the family graves, of course – they wouldn't appreciate a cuckoo in the nest. The poor souls who had drowned yesterday wouldn't be buried here, though. There were too many of them; more than 200, he'd heard the mayor say on the radio just now – she'd appealed for coffins. They'd be shipped off to Sicily unless their relatives claimed them. Fat chance of that happening, he said, scratching the white stubble on his chin.

He led the optician to a plot around the corner, wheezing as he walked, his callused heels in his flip-flops split as deeply as the dry earth. 'Buried him a few weeks back,' he said gruffly, rubbing his rough hand over a large grey patch of concrete at the top of a stack. 'Young boy. About seventeen they reckon. Probably Eritrean. Drowned in a dinghy.'

The optician edged forward. The Eritrean boy was sharing his vault with a moustachioed man who looked out sternly from his photograph in a petrol-coloured suit and navy tie. A pastel painting of the Madonna looked down on the moustachioed man protectively and over his right shoulder two fluttering *putti* had been carved onto the stonework, watching him with adoration. The careful attention to detail rendered the blankness of the crude cement patch above him truly pathetic. It looked, thought the optician, as if the boy had been deliberately effaced, censored from existence.

The gravedigger seemed to know what he was thinking. 'I might not know his name,' he growled fiercely. 'But I remember him. Believe me, I remember them all.'

The wind had begun to amuse itself by picking up plastic watering cans and bouquets of dead flowers, racing them along the narrow alleyways between the gravestones and then flinging them to the ground, where they spun exhausted on the grit walkways.

A large piece of jagged white plastic was cartwheeling towards them and the gravedigger stopped it with his foot. He picked it up and cursed. 'It was loose and now the wind's torn it off the grave,' he spat, thrusting it at the optician and stumping off furiously.

The optician looked at the flimsy plastic panel and read what he could of the incomplete inscription.

Here lies the body of an unknown –
Drowned off the coast of Lampe—
Believed to be from the Horn of A—
He was aged around twenty.

He found the gravedigger in front of a marble mausoleum where he was propping up the remaining half of the panel with a pot of borrowed flowers and a small rock of old concrete. The wind had made a spiteful job of tearing the cheap plastic board in two.

'Why are they left to rot like this?' asked the optician incredulously. 'Why does no one care for them?'

The gravedigger wheeled round quickly and snarled at the optician, his eyes wide with anger. 'Why are they left to *die* like this?' he snapped. 'You answer me *that* question!'

He snatched the shard of plastic from the optician and waved it at him. 'Why does Europe do the minimum possible to stop this? You tell me that!' He rolled his r's dramatically. 'God knows it makes me *furious!*'

The optician could not answer him. He held the plastic panel together while the gravedigger blocked the two halves in with the pot and a couple of rocks. The optician stared at the fractured plaque. Unknown and uncared for. These people seemed to be no one's problem.

The gravedigger pressed his palm flat against the stone. 'Each time you bury one, you hope it's the last,' he said. 'You always hope it will be the last.' He picked up his pail of plaster, nodded politely to the optician and trudged off, sighing.

It felt suddenly cold in the graveyard and the optician decided to cut his run short and head home. He was still physically spent from yesterday and the nervous energy that had been fuelling him until now was beginning to cool in his veins, leaving him feeling heavy-limbed and slightly queasy. As he jogged slowly back to the port, he thought of the gravedigger's words.

Why wasn't more being done to stop these tragedies? It had been pure chance that *Galata* had been in the right place at more or less the right time. Yet everyone knew these refugee boats kept travelling to Lampedusa and Sicily, so why weren't there professional search and rescue teams on permanent duty?

His head, normally calm and empty on this homeward stretch, was teeming with questions.

Maria and Francesco were in the shop with Teresa when he got back and they fell on him when he entered the door.

'We've been invited to a service tomorrow!' beamed Teresa. 'The mayor's office called to invite us all – we'll be able to see them again – they'll all be there.' She took his hand and squeezed it. 'We can see them again!'

Francesco filled in the details; he had jotted notes down on a scrap of paper. It was to be a service of remembrance and reflection in a hangar at the airport where the coffins were being stored. All the survivors would be there; all the rescue workers were to attend as well as the mayor and some politicians. It was to be a brief service before the bodies were transferred to Sicily and there would be a minute's silence to honour the dead.

Maria was emotional. 'And can you believe it,' she said, 'Our government in Rome has announced each of the dead is to be given a state funeral!' She smiled at Teresa. 'We've been talking about it just now – it's a sign that everything is going to change.'

The optician smiled back at them thinly. He thought of the cheap plastic panel, sheared off by the wind on the grave of the drowned young migrant and of all the nameless, trampled wooden crosses that the bindweed seemed determined to suffocate. A state funeral was truly a grand gesture. The grand gesture of a guilty conscience. He tried to imagine the coffins draped in the red, white and green of the Italian flag, a military band playing while soldiers carried the caskets to a well-chosen spot in a shady graveyard to lay them to rest in their own mausoleum together. Call him cynical, but he couldn't imagine it. He just couldn't.

Chapter 9

The optician had always associated the airport with excitement. Didn't everybody? For him and for Teresa the airport meant catching a plane back to Naples to see the boys – it meant family dinners, laughter and fun. Holidays.

There wasn't a breath of laughter left now. *Galata*'s crew walked to the airport hangar together in silence, their arms linked. They were all desperate to see the people they had saved, but terrified too of seeing the coffins. Teresa was worried that she would not recognize those they had helped; how rude and dismissive it would seem, she had said to her husband, if she could not pick out their faces from all the other migrants! He was cursing the fact that he did not speak English or whatever language they spoke. He wanted to explain to them that they had tried so hard to get to see them before now, that they had been worrying about them, that they had repeatedly called the hospital for news of those who had needed treatment. But how did you convey the message 'we have never stopped thinking of you' in sign language? They didn't possess enough English between them to explain that it was the complex bureaucracy of migration rules that had prevented them from coming to visit the survivors in the reception centre. He was so anxious that they should understand how hard they had tried, that they had not forgotten them for one second.

But in the event there was no awkwardness. The migrants were waiting for them, watching for them outside the entrance to the hangar, and as they approached, they ran to them eagerly like primary school children meeting their parents at the end of the school day, clamouring for them with their arms outstretched. The women folded them against their chests and rocked them. Big men, some nearly two metres tall, cuddling as little boys do, their heads bent on Teresa's shoulder, nestled on Maria's neck, weeping.

He had never been good at reaching out to people. He was not one of those types who touched people while talking to them, laying a hand on a knee or a shoulder. Teresa always said he was so uncomfortable at physical contact with strangers that he could appear cold. Yet when the first young man had taken his hand and squeezed it tight in thanks, it hadn't been enough; it had felt insipid. So the optician had forcibly pulled the boy towards him and locked him in a fierce embrace. He hadn't wanted to let the boy go. He hadn't wanted to let any of them go.

It didn't matter they didn't share a language. They seemed to understand how worried *Galata*'s crew had been as to how they were faring. Some gave them the thumbs-up sign to reassure them they were OK, then inclined their head on their open palm to indicate they were just very tired. One of the teenagers took the optician's hand and held it over his breast so that the optician could feel the thumping of his heart. He smiled at the optician and pointed his finger at him. The optician understood the message. You gave me life, he was saying. You gave me my life.

He told them his name and they rolled the strange syllables around their mouths shyly, tasting the sound. They told him theirs, but there were so many of them that he caught only the melody of them and not the form. He tried to count them as they lined up respectfully to embrace Francesco.

They recognized that Francesco, as the eldest, was the boss and they understood that it had been his boat that had saved them. Father, they said, as they kissed his hand. Our father.

They were wearing incongruous clothes for this solemn occasion. The reception centre had obviously kitted them out with whatever they had had and they looked almost as raggedy as they had on *Galata*. Trousers hung loosely from their narrow hips, held up by stringy bits of blue nylon cord, and many were wearing T-shirts proclaiming allegiance to Italian football teams which the optician doubted they'd ever heard of. Most were in trainers, but those who'd clearly been at the back of the queue had had to make do with the left-over mis-matched flip-flops. One forlorn man was wearing a pair of ladies' furry bedroom slippers with the pompom missing from the right foot. In another life, thought the optician, it might have been funny. Right now it was so pathetic that he wanted to take off his own shoes and offer the man his dignity.

Thirteen thousand asylum-seekers had arrived in Italy so far this year – Gabriele had told them that when he'd come to fetch them in the car to take them to the aircraft hangar. Until now it had just been a random, meaningless figure, an empty statistic. Yet here they were before them, flesh and blood, bone and gristle, with the salt of their tears mingling with their own. Boys with names that sounded like music, men whose hearts thumped with life and promise. Names not numbers! Names!

There were a handful of women survivors by the door, but he recognized the girl they'd saved immediately because of her long braids; they splayed out from under a small black scarf she had placed over her head. A long black shirt had replaced her turquoise T-shirt, but she still wore her old look of pride. He wanted to hold her, but it was clear she was terrified of anyone coming close.

When Elena tried to hug her, she voiced her gratitude politely and sincerely, both in English and Italian, but stood stiffly in Elena's arms and did not allow herself to be scooped into an embrace the way the men did. What force she must have to keep back the tears! He, Matteo, Francesco and Gabriele could do nothing to temper their emotions.

It was Maria who spotted the girl's hands. She had seen her discomfort at being held too close, so when it was her turn to speak to her, she had simply taken her hands in hers. The girl had winced in pain. When Maria had lifted the girl's hands to examine them, Maria had cried out herself. The pads of each of her fingers were singed red and black and bulbous yellow blisters sat on top of the deep burns.

'Who hurt you, darling, who hurt you?' asked Maria, her voice panicky, her hand touching the woman's face.

The girl shrugged and pulled a lighter and the remnants of a supermarket carrier bag from her jeans pocket.

'No fingerprints, please,' she explained with an embarrassed smile. 'Please, no fingerprints.'

He was heartsick at what she had done. He had read in the paper that migrants sometimes tried to destroy their fingerprints, but he had never thought through what that actually meant. It was to get around some EU rule that demanded refugees must claim asylum in the first safe country they arrived in. Few people wanted to stay in jobless Italy though, so naturally they headed north. But if the authorities caught them in another country and their fingerprints were found on a database, they could be shunted straight back from where they had started. He winced looking at the swollen blisters. He asked Teresa if she had a tube of arnica in her bag, forgetting for a second that the boys had long grown up and Teresa had no need to carry comforters for them any more.

He held the girl gently by the wrists and studied her burnt hands, shaking his head. He recalled suddenly the image of that horrible doll he had trodden on in the grass outside the reception centre, with its trampled, battered face and bleeding battery cavity. The brutality of this whole damned system! Hadn't these people suffered enough, weren't they sufficiently damaged without having to resort to this? He was too distressed to say anything to the young woman. He would have liked to have asked her where she was planning to go and whether she had family there waiting for her, but he couldn't trust his voice to stay strong. He looked her in the eye for a long moment, hoping she would know that he wished her well, that he was telling her he would never forget her. She melted away from him.

Inside the hangar, the uniform coffins were spaced out with military precision, each exactly one metre from its neighbour. On the lid of every burnished mahogany casket a single red rose had been laid. There were over a hundred of them. And fronting the sickening parade were four tiny white coffins. They were each decorated with a small, smiling teddy bear in a blue-and-white striped T-shirt with a love heart on the centre of its chest. In two of those caskets lay the toddlers wearing brand new patent leather shoes. Number 92 and number 14. The optician pulled at a loose thread on the sleeve cuff of his jacket and twisted the thread around his finger tightly. He did not think he would have the courage to stay for the service.

Matteo was staring at the far wall of the hangar, plucking nervously at his beard. The optician noticed he would not look at the caskets. Just before the service started, Matteo leant over and whispered, 'Last week, before we rescued these people, did you know that thirteen people drowned off the coast of Sicily? I barely registered the news. I barely gave them a thought.'

So he was not alone, then, in feeling this guilt.

For the remembrance service they were asked to stand with the members of the emergency services, with the coastguard and the fishermen who had joined the rescue efforts. He was glad of that now, looking at the migrants as they faced the coffins. Some were bent double with grief, squatting on the floor, their heads between their knees, while three of the surviving women were keening the terrible death wail that they had heard from the boat. This ceremony was theirs; it was for those who had died and for those who had survived, and it would have felt intrusive to be standing in the middle of such profound, personal grief. He could hear Teresa gasping as she tried to temper her own distress and he dared not look at her as he took her hand. He was thankful the television cameras had not been allowed inside to film this intimate moment.

He tried to concentrate on the service, breathing in the musky scent of incense and the wisps of smoke from the candles. An imam and a Catholic priest were taking turns to sing verses and to chant prayers, their voices sounding thin and reedy as they bounced off the immense walls of the huge aircraft hangar. And although he didn't believe in any of this religious stuff, he felt something stir inside him at the beauty of the haunting sounds and the solemnity of it all. It felt holy and pure and unique. He would stay. He would make himself stay. He owed the migrants that.

There must have been two or three hundred people circled around the coffins, yet how tiny and insignificant they seemed in all this space! He imagined the men in suits must be politicians from Rome and Sicily. They stood like soldiers with their backs exaggeratedly straight, mumbling responses to the prayers, occasionally crossing themselves. Their own mayor had her face buried in a handkerchief and the optician could see her whole body was shaking.

It sounded like poetry when the priest read out the long list of the dead. Exotic names that washed up over his head like waves so that he couldn't tell where one name ended and a new one began. Efrem, Asmeret, Gaim, Biniam, Niyat, Senait. Somewhere in the world, mothers would be polishing framed photographs of these lost sons and daughters, waiting anxiously for a phone call to reassure them that they had arrived safely.

He watched the woman he'd rescued blowing on her painful fingers. What was her name? Was her brother in one of the caskets? He imagined the two of them plotting, mustering the courage to take this adventure together, taking comfort in the knowledge that whatever happened on the journey, at least they would be together to pursue their dreams in this new and promised land.

He forced himself to look at the forlorn survivors. They would have visualized only positive things for their new life in the place they thought was Paradise. Everything was to be fresh and exciting in Europe and they would have expected only laughter and jobs, safe homes and freedom. Now, he could see that fable unwinding and peeling away from them like the coloured paint on the cracked hulls of the wrecks he had seen rotting by the port. He squeezed his eyes shut to try to stop the tears. He felt useless. Yes, he had saved them, but for what kind of future? All their delightful fantasies had curdled and spoilt and they did not know how to create a new dream to believe in. No one had told them that in Europe, in Paradise, people also suffered and were wretched.

He became conscious that one of the young men he had rescued was watching him. He hastily wiped the sleeve of his jacket over his eyes. The teenager continued to look at him, his mouth slightly open. It was the same desperately expectant look that they had all given him when they were in the water. Save me. Help me. Please.

The optician clasped his hands together. Was he praying? Is this what prayer was? He glanced at Francesco, whose head was bent low. He wasn't sure if Francesco was a believer. They'd never talked about things like that. Gabriele was biting his knuckles. He looked feverish. Giulia was whispering words, her fingers pulling hard at her dangling turtle earrings. He took Teresa's candle from her – she was sobbing so much that the hot wax was dropping onto her hand and burning her. She kept asking him the same question: were the police sure who the children's mothers were so they could be buried together? She was so distressed to see the little coffins apart like that – the mothers wouldn't want to be separated from their children, she kept insisting, they ought to be placed side by side.

He had not told Teresa what the police diver had said about finding the drowned woman hugging her little ones to her body, about the children's new shoes. He did his best to reassure her, but what did he know? He suspected it would be mostly guesswork and that the unnamed would be buried beside strangers in a country they had dreamt of but had never got the chance to know.

All day the divers had been under the water again, harvesting corpses, sorting through the jumble of tangled limbs on the dark seabed and tying the bodies together with rigging rope before dragging them back up to the light. He had gone to the port to buy prawns from the fishmonger's, but afterwards he had turned right instead of left, drawn back in spite of himself to the little strip of coarse sand that faced the coastguard's landing strip. It wasn't prurience; he still clung to the ludicrous hope that someone would have been found alive and that he could go home to Teresa to tell her some good news. He wanted desperately to give his wife some good news. But as he'd crossed through the shipbuilding yard and onto the patch of rough beach, he'd seen the hunched figure of the police diver sitting on the breakwater, his arms crossed protectively over his head as if to ward off blows, his back sporadically hiccupping. Respectfully, he'd backed away.

The service was coming to an end now, and thank God because he needed air.

Perhaps tomorrow, perhaps right now, another rickety, unseaworthy boat was being stuffed with frightened migrants on the Libyan coast and was making its uncertain way to Lampedusa. He swallowed. And how many of them would make it?

As they were filing out, he felt a sudden desperation to get away from all this death, from these coffins and this heart-wrenching pervasive sadness that he could do nothing about. He wanted to run home to rewind the tape of the past few days, to press Pause at the point at which they had all boarded *Galata* and to erase that part and put another scene in its place. *Aperitivo* at that awful loud bar Matteo liked, a humble picnic down at Rabbit Beach, a pistachio ice cream at Francesco's daughter's place! Anything, anything but this . . .

Teresa pulled back on his arm. He knew she would have stopped to say goodbye to the four little white coffins. He turned back with her. The teddies smiled cheerfully at them, oblivious.

They were not given long to say goodbye to the refugees after the service. The police wanted them back in the reception centre quickly, but so many were reluctant to leave their dead; two of the women had to be prised off the coffin lids, they were still wailing their sorrow as they were escorted to the police van.

It was indescribable, the parting from them. The roar of the emotion inside him frightened the optician; he did not feel in control. As they hugged goodbye, he was aware of hearing strange animalistic noises and even afterwards, when he was back home and distanced from it all, he was not sure if the cries had come from Francesco, one of the others, or from himself. He just wanted to save them. From whatever came next, he wanted to save them.

The survivors spoke urgently in their own language and in snatches of English, clutching at them, clinging to them. He understood nothing except the words 'thank you'. But he could sense what they wanted to say.

As the police van backed out of the car park, its headlights caught them full in the face. For a brief second he saw the crumpled faces of Gabriele and Francesco and the wet tracks coursing down Matteo's cheeks. It was the first time he had ever seen his friends cry.

They sat up late that night, he and Teresa. You can't sleep after something like that. The last three days had been the most emotionally intense experience of his entire life, of all of their lives. His wife looked battered by the shock and he supposed he did too; one of his customers that morning had asked him if he were ill. He hadn't exactly led a charmed life, he'd suffered his own losses, had had his own moments of pain, but he had had no idea that such profound depths of sorrow existed. He could never imagine feeling such an acute sadness again.

Teresa wanted to see the news and he switched on the television reluctantly, not wanting her to be exposed again to the awful images of the coffins. He started in his chair. The police diver to whom he'd been talking the day before was being interviewed on the quayside with the arms of his diving buddies draped protectively around his shoulders.

This evening, the diver was saying falteringly, wedged right into the prow of the sunken ship, he had found a very young woman clutching a bundle of rags. He had swum over to her and when he pulled at the bundle, the cloth had fallen away to reveal a tiny baby boy. His mask had fogged up with tears, continued the diver, and he had nearly choked. Because he realized the baby was still attached to his mother by the umbilical cord.

How naive he'd been, thought the optician, how naive. Because there would always be greater sorrow, deeper and more unfathomable than any of us could ever imagine.

Chapter 10

The optician worried about Teresa's nightmares. More than two weeks had passed since they had rescued those people at sea and the nightmares seemed to be getting worse with time, not better. They had all had them; they'd been quite open with each other about the effects of the trauma on their mental states. Gabriele admitted he was suffering from insomnia; his skin was permanently the colour of tracing paper now and his denim-blue eyes looked bleached and faded. Elena, Matteo and Francesco were struggling with their anger: Elena had rowed with her boss on the telephone; Matteo had blown up at his girlfriend and called things off. Giulia and Maria felt down and depressed. Maria seemed to shrink into herself, hunkering down into the folds of her fishing-net scarf, while Giulia's wayward hair had become unkempt and wild. But Teresa's suffering was truly terrible. She'd wake up choking, not able to breathe, sobbing and clutching at imaginary figures.

They'd had to go the hospital in the middle of the night last week. Panic attacks, the doctor had said. They had certainly panicked him. She needed to talk it out with someone, but he found it so difficult reliving those awful hours on the water. Once she had been so distracted that she had appeared in the shop in her dressing gown. She had looked at him curiously when he had hurried her towards the staircase – as if he was someone she knew yet couldn't quite place. When he'd pressed upon her the impropriety of coming downstairs in her nightwear, when he'd tried to explain that it would have been truly embarrassing for them both if a client had been in the shop when she'd appeared like that, she had just searched his face with her emerald green eyes as if she were trying to decipher a deeper message.

He didn't tell her, but the shipwreck played in his own head when he slept like a cine film on a loop. The pictures were in glorious Technicolor, but the most terrifying thing was that the images were completely silent. He could see migrants begging for help and he could see Francesco with his mouth stretched wide, yelling something at him. But he couldn't hear what anyone was saying – he couldn't even hear the sea – so he just stood there, frozen, not knowing what to do, while the heads sank under the waves.

If he was honest, these images didn't just come to him at night.

The problem was the grief just would not go away. The coffins had been removed to Sicily and almost all of the survivors had been transferred to the mainland, but the sadness lingered on the island like the wispy October fog which crept in from the sea each morning, its damp fingers chilling and pervasive.

And a new source of sorrow had arrived to fill the vacuum left by the coffins. Relatives of the dead and missing had come to Lampedusa to identify bodies and to try to establish if their family members had indeed been on that fateful boat. They sat hunched in the cafés and bars of the island: the lucky migrants who had already made it to Europe and who had benevolently funded the ill-fated journeys of the dead.

At lunch-time the relatives kept watch outside the *carabinieri* station near the optician's shop, throwing themselves on anyone in uniform who went in or out, pressing them for information and pushing photographs of their missing relatives into the policemen's hands. He'd seen some of them standing at the gates by Porto Favaloro, stalking the quayside, ready to pounce on the police divers and the search and rescue crews when they docked. They followed the police and the divers to the cafés and the bars too. Once, while he and Teresa were having their morning coffee, he had seen a police diver hesitate looking at a photograph that was pushed urgently in front of his face as he sat eating breakfast with a colleague. The diver had wiped the greasy *arancini* from his face with a tissue and had taken the picture and studied it closely, whispering conspiratorially with his colleague. They had left the food uneaten then and had gently led the woman with the photograph out of the bar and into their pick-up truck outside, presumably to take her to the morgue. But mostly the police and the divers just scratched their chins before shaking their heads apologetically and walking away.

The migrants sat in Francesco's ice-cream parlour too, frantic. From his bar stool at the counter, the optician watched them shouting into mobile phones in their own languages, in English, in Arabic, Italian and in German. Their tables were strewn with photographs and tatty pieces of paper. They ended calls dejectedly and scored through phone numbers on their notepads or paper napkins, jotting down new ones and scribbling notes.

A young African man in trendy ripped jeans noticed Francesco's and the optician's concern and came over to introduce himself. He was a language student at Munich university, he said, and although he had left Eritrea with his parents when he'd been a baby, he had felt it his duty to come to Lampedusa to help the relatives search and to translate for them. They were calling the traffickers, he explained, nodding to the relatives, to see if their niece, nephew or missing cousin had been a passenger on that boat. He translated conversations for them in a low whisper.

'He was probably wearing a denim jacket,' shouted one man hopelessly, pushing his reading glasses onto the top of his head and rubbing his eyes. 'And he has a crescent-shaped scar on his left cheek.' He held the photograph to the light. 'No, wait! He has the scar on his right cheek. Do you remember him boarding at Misrata? He's eighteen, but maybe looks a bit older.'

Some were well dressed and clearly educated. The optician's eye spotted the well-cut lines of a beige Armani jacket on an African woman of near enough his own age who kept pausing her conversations with the traffickers to take business calls in Italian on another mobile phone.

'Her mum says she always wore a ring in the shape of a coiled snake. Does that jog your memory at all? We haven't heard from her in two weeks now and we believe she was heading to Misrata. Please?'

The optician almost wished the student would stop translating for them. To hear these desperate people having to ask favours from unfeeling criminals turned his stomach. He sipped his espresso.

The captain of the boat had been arrested. Some of the migrants they had saved had recognized him at the reception centre and reported him to the police. He was a Tunisian, apparently, who had already been deported once from Italy and was part of a large trafficking ring. The migrants said they'd been beaten for complaining about the claustrophobic conditions on board the boat. When some of the women had not been able to come up with the whole fare that was being demanded from them, they'd been raped in part-payment. The optician had read that this morning, leaning over Francesco's shoulder, scanning the paper on the bar's counter. Francesco had read it too, obviously. He lifted his eyebrows to the optician, and said simply: 'The girl. The girl we rescued.'

More than 350 corpses had now been recovered and the police diving teams were still looking. There had been another shipwreck that week between Malta and Lampedusa: Syrians this time, and Palestinians. Thirty-four of them had drowned before the coastguard could get to them. The optician twisted the elastic top of his sock and let it snap back. This stretch of the Mediterranean between Lampedusa and Libya was turning into a graveyard.

Yesterday morning he'd been at the fishmonger's when the night boats had come in with their haul, and while he was waiting for his fish to be wrapped, he had chatted politely to the fishermen as they unloaded, asking them whether they'd had a good catch. One of the fishermen had taken off his oilskin and told him he couldn't take the stress any more, profit or no profit. He was going to retire early and move to Palermo, he explained, to be with his son's family. It wasn't just the fear that he'd find himself out at sea in the middle of a migrant shipwreck, he said, it was the fear of what he might find in his nets when he pulled them up.

The man with the reading glasses sitting near the bar counter hung up his phone and slumped forward in his chair, his elbows on the table, his head in his hands. They didn't need the Eritrean student to tell them it was bad news. The optician looked away quickly. Maybe if they had been faster out there on the sea, maybe if he'd clocked that screaming more quickly, this poor man would never have had to come to Lampedusa and undertake such a hideous task. His relative would have been safe on *Galata*'s deck, with the girls all fussing over him and finding him clothes and water. He kicked the leg of his bar stool. Why had the coastguard made them stop? Why had they been made to turn their backs? He was sure they could have saved more. He rubbed the pulsating vein above his right ear. But one boat had passed those desperate people and had not stopped at all. How did that boat's crew sleep at night?

The woman in the Armani jacket raised her voice and was thumping the table in frustration as she talked on the phone.

'Sounds like the trafficker wants more money for the information,' sighed the student. 'He seems to be telling her he *might* have information, but she'll need to help him out a bit.'

It was all so ugly. There and here too. The state funeral that had been promised for the dead had been downgraded to a 'solemn ceremony' in Agrigento; the survivors had not even been invited. There was no special memorial mausoleum for the drowned; they had been scattered in cemeteries across Sicily, and who knew where those who had been buried without names were lying now? They had been found in the depths of the sea, brought back into the light – but on land they had been lost again.

And the survivors? The optician rubbed his hands up and down the legs of his trousers. He felt sick when he thought about the survivors and their future. A couple of them had taken Francesco's email address, but there'd been no news of them so far. The optician could see Francesco fiddling with the computer now; if challenged, he'd say he was checking stuff for his carpentry work, but the optician knew what his friend was looking for. Poor Francesco. Every time they met, he'd look at him expectantly and Francesco would sigh and shake his head.

There had been rumours that the survivors could be fined

thousands of euros for entering Italy illegally. Fined! Which planet did these lawmakers come from? The prime minister had come to Lampedusa only the other day and visited the reception centre. He must have seen the desperate state these migrants were in. The centre was bulging and running at three or four times its capacity; some refugees had to sleep outdoors. He thought of the pitiful man they'd rescued who had been wearing the ladies' bedroom slippers at the memorial service. Where did the politicians imagine he had secreted his supposed wealth to pay such a fine? These people had nothing – they were totally bereft. They did not even have their dream to cling to any more.

Francesco passed him another espresso and playfully punched his cheek. The optician attempted a smile. He wasn't stupid; he knew that Europe couldn't possibly welcome every single person who fancied a better life for himself, but there had to be some alternative to this mess. He knew from his internet research that most Eritreans who arrived in Europe were automatically granted asylum; abject poverty, years of war and a military dictatorship were hard for any EU country to argue against. So why make them go through this treacherous journey, then? It was like a sinister selection test: manage this deadly assault course successfully and bingo! you've earned yourself a place in Paradise. Matteo teased him that he sounded like a politician when he talked like that, He should run for mayor, he'd joked drily when they'd met for a beer last week. But the optician hated politics. Politics was all about self-interest. This wasn't about politics anyway; it was about humanitarianism. It was about anticipating the desperate hands in the water and acting before they got there.

The woman in the smart jacket collected her things together from the table and stuffed them into her canvas travel bag. She approached the bar and settled her bill with Francesco. Gently, he wished her luck with her search.

'I have to fly back to Rome in a couple of hours,' she said in perfect Italian, shaking her head. She unzipped the top of her bag and pulled out a photograph.

'I'm looking for her,' she said, handing the photo to Francesco. He tilted it so the optician could see the picture too.

It was a headshot of a pretty girl in her late teens or very early twenties with close-cropped hair and a wide, red-lipsticked smile. She was wearing a pale blue, low-cut satin blouse, a lot of make-up and a silver crucifix dangled in her cleavage.

The woman looked at the picture fondly. 'She's my second cousin. This picture was taken a couple of years ago when she was at home in Asmara,' she explained. 'There was a family party because she had a week's leave from the military.'

Francesco muttered some appropriately kind comments. The woman shrugged. 'I haven't seen her since she was five,' she explained. 'I send her family money a few times a year and her mum sends me photographs by way of return. I sent her the funds to flee Eritrea and her uncle in Sweden wired what she needed for the boat crossing from Libya. That's where she was heading, you see, to Sweden. We're almost certain she was in the boat that sank.'

She shuddered. The police had asked her to study some photographs of the drowned women, but their faces were so puffy and swollen with water that she had not liked to linger on the images. In any case, she had not recognized her cousin.

The optician scrutinized the laughing girl in the picture again. Done up to the nines like that, it was easy to imagine her about to head off for an evening out in Naples or Palermo, perhaps on a date with a boyfriend. She did not look like a pitiful refugee, she just looked ordinary – the type of good-looking girl you passed on the street all the time. She had just been born in the wrong place, poor kid.

He handed the woman back the photograph and asked her awkwardly, his eyes lowered, what her cousin was called.

'Saba,' said the woman 'Her name is Saba.'

A pretty name, Saba, the optician said quietly. He would have liked to be able to turn to the woman, to touch her arm and to say to her, yes, I remember this girl! I saved her. I pulled your cousin onto my boat. Instead, he swivelled away from her on his bar stool and twisted the elastic of his sock more tightly around his finger as Francesco began to unpack the glasses from the dishwasher.

No, he had not saved Saba. And he had not saved the man with a crescent-shaped scar on his right cheek. He had not saved the thirteen men who washed up on Sicily's coast a couple of weeks back and he had never once wondered whether one of them had had a distinguishing mark or if another was wearing a ring cast in the form of a sleeping snake. He had let their deaths wash over him and then retreat back out to sea and sink without a trace.

The woman put the photograph back in her bag, zipped it up and headed for the door.

'I'm sorry!' blurted the optician suddenly, turning to face her. 'I'm so sorry that –'

The woman stopped and looked at him for a long moment, confused. Then her face cleared and, heaving her bag onto her shoulder, she nodded briefly at the optician and left.

That night he dreamt he was alone on a rowing boat and that the water below him was thundering and thrashing as some huge sea-beast reared up alongside the boat. He clung to the wooden sides, but they felt as flimsy as ice-lolly sticks and as they snapped in his hands he could see thick coils of silver scales swishing through the holes in the boat, and he knew that at any moment the head of a giant serpent would emerge from the waves and bear down on him. And then a man with a scar on his right cheek appeared beside him, blowing a whistle saying it was over. It was over.

He woke up to Teresa's screaming.

Chapter 11

Galata was fretful in the harbour, creaking and see-sawing with the other boats, pulling on her mooring as the buffeting wind unsettled the sea beneath her. The optician watched her straining to break free of the marina and understood her. Like them, she had been turned back before she was ready; like them, she had left a job half-finished. He imagined she was yearning to be back in the open water to pick up the search again. He stroked her keel roughly as he might pet a dog. It was over, the coastguard captain had signalled, crossing and uncrossing his arms. It was over. But it would never be over for them.

He had told Teresa he was going to the post office. It was not exactly a lie; he had that faulty batch of contact lenses he needed to ship back to Naples and there were some cheques that needed sending, but he knew that as soon as this was done he would wind up here at the port to spend a quiet moment with *Galata*. He told himself that he was doing it for Francesco. He'd check on the boat to give Francesco peace of mind now that he was back in Milan in the carpentry workshop. Yes, it was for Francesco that he'd come.

There was no one else about. The sullen afternoon sun, choked behind a catarrh of heavy clouds, strained to pick out a few steely glints from the light-starved water that looked thick and murky. Even the fresh white paint of *Galata*'s cabin seemed grubby in the dirty light. He stepped tentatively onto her deck and felt her rock beneath his weight. She had been stripped for the winter – her cushions, flares, fenders and dock lines all stored inside out of the way of the elements. Her gunwale gaped where the lifebuoy was usually attached. He looked down at the stern step and his hands immediately clenched into fists.

He was lonely without Francesco. He was lonely without them – he could see them all again now as he scanned *Galata*'s deck. The girl in the oil- slicked turquoise T-shirt sitting aloof there at the bow like a tragic figurehead. The teenage boy who'd made a nappy out of Teresa's red T-shirt, sobbing as he'd traced with his oily finger the number of passengers for them on the wooden boards. Here, on *Galata*'s deck, the migrants had all been safe. Now he feared they would be clutching at long, tangled lines of slippery asylum bureaucracy and that their grip would never be sure again. The email that Francesco had eventually received from one of the young men had been confused and unnerving. They were in a big holding camp in Sicily, the boy had said, and they had each been given a number. The optician sat down on the hard bench and hooked his finger over the elastic top of his sock, letting it snap back against his anklebone. Camps and numbers did not give him peace of mind.

He ran the ball of his thumb along the gunwale, remembering how the bones of their knuckles had jutted out as they had clung there in shock. He needed them around him. He had come to understand that somehow, when their hands had locked into his, it wasn't just them who had been pulled back into life. Up there on the cabin roof he had opened his eyes wide and seen them for the first time: the black dots that were not black dots, but men, women and children – flesh and bone and blood. He had stared into their eyes, which were rolling on the very cusp between life and death and he had not seen strangers. He had recognized their need and he had understood. He had begun to see.

He rubbed the tip of his trainer against an encrusted seagull dropping on the scrubbed deck and the rubber toecap juddered against the wood and sent pins and needles shooting up his calf and set his teeth on edge. All his senses seemed to be overly sharpened these days. At lunchtime he had not been able to eat the chickpeas in the salad Teresa had made because he could taste the aluminium of the can on their skin; they were the same brand they always used, she had protested, fishing the tin from the bin to show him, but the metallic tang coated his tongue like blood and he could not swallow them. When she'd clanged the bin lid back down in frustration and thrown the salad servers into the sink, he'd flinched at the ringing noise that echoed through the kitchen. He took off his glasses and pressed the heels of his hands into his eyes.

Teresa seemed to float through the days, numbed. She drifted in and out of the apartment in a daze, walking into the bedroom to pick something up and then forgetting what it was and stumbling out again with the unsteady and confused gait of a sleepwalker. The doctor said she was suffering from deep shock; they'd had to visit the hospital several times. She looked at everything now with a detached interest as if it didn't really figure or matter much in her own world.

He imagined her thoughts were piling up upon themselves like the marbled white beach stones that filled the decorative glass jar in the bathroom. Somehow she was managing to weight down the most terrible thoughts at the bottom, but what would happen to her if the stones suddenly shifted? He felt frightened for her. If he was honest, he felt a little frightened of her too. He had always known who Teresa was and how she would react. She would cry when he was sharp with her; she would light up when he told her one of the boys was on the phone; she would blush like a schoolgirl again when he whispered to her over a crowded dinner table that she looked beautiful. But since that day on the water she had become as unreadable as a cat. She slinked around the apartment, not needing him, and it made him nervous.

He needed her help more downstairs in the shop. He kept forgetting things like the courtesy calls and the paperwork was getting muddled. He had done nothing about marking down the sunglasses for an end-of-season sale. He knew he'd make a loss on those frames now; last year that would have kept him awake at night doing the mental arithmetic, and although he tried to concern himself with it, he could not make it matter any more. He hadn't looked at the accounts for a week.

A few journalists still circled like vultures. The red-haired reporter had come round to his shop yesterday when he was out, hounding Teresa, offering money for the 'exclusive story'. He had been deeply offended about the money when Teresa had told him. Is that how people saw him? A ruthless opportunist who would trade the testimonies of the desperate for a few gold pieces?

And he despised the pejorative word 'story' they used to describe the tragedy. It made the shipwreck seem like a once-upon-a-time fable that you might tell to children at bedtime. He picked at a speck of white paint on the metal gunwale. Well, there would be no happily ever after, not for the dead, not for the survivors, not for them.

He and Teresa were the only ones left on the island now. The little gathering Francesco organized every year to say goodbye to the group had been subdued this time, although the optician noticed they all drank more wine than usual. Elena had got tetchy with an inattentive waiter and Matteo's clowning had been forced and half-hearted so that only the good-natured Maria had continued to laugh. Everyone's face bore the heavy, dark traces of their disturbed nights. The pouches under Giulia's eyes were so pronounced he had asked her if a mosquito had bitten her. She'd become very teary during the meal. After they'd eaten, he, Francesco and Gabriele had sat on the terrace smoking endless cigarettes together. They said very little, but the silence was comforting and companionable. Just the eight of them. Just the eight.

He decided to text Francesco from his phone, to tell him the old lady was doing fine. He'd make out they'd just been strolling, he and Teresa, just taking a walk by the quayside when they'd made a quick detour to check up on *Galata* after the recent rainstorm. All good, he texted. Everything's good here, fine and dandy. Francesco's reply came back quickly. Are you OK? he asked.

He felt foolish really, but he climbed up on the roof of the wheelhouse anyway. Back to his old lookout post. His eyes smarted as he strained to look down deep into the harbour's water. A shoal of small silvery blue fish flitted between the snugged boats, discernible only intermittently as they zigzagged through the shards of sporadic sunlight. He took off his glasses and let the images around him blur and the colours bleed and run into one another. The myopic world was a softer one, an indistinct jumble of shapes and forms with no edges.

But he could not ignore the fact that the waving hands had always been visible to him. They had waved in the water, yes, but they had also waved from the reception centre, from the church steps and from the roadside where he had jogged past them, blindly. They had waved from the newspaper columns and from the television screens where he had filtered them out and switched them off. They had always been in his line of vision and he had chosen not to see them.

He checked his watch and realized he'd have to walk back smartly to make his four o'clock appointment at the shop. He grimaced. Mr Abate, the crabby old boatman who rented out a fleet of pedalos to the tourists in high season, was never exactly a pleasure to see. He swung himself down from the cabin roof and stood silently for a moment or two, listening to the boat's complaining, before climbing back onto the quayside.

On the way home, he crossed over the road to pause at the migrant boat graveyard where a flotilla of wooden cadavers lay marooned on the gravel, their hulls splintered with unsightly wounds. The worn-out vessels were lying heavily on their sides as if in a gesture of surrender. He winced as he looked at them. For how many years now had desperate people washed up here, drained of every last drop of their strength? He clenched his jaw. And how many more smashed wrecks would it take before Europe stopped debating and instead agreed to do something? The cawing gulls, wheeling and gliding on the warm thermals, tormented his ears.

Mr Abate was early for his appointment, and when the optician walked into the shop he was already grumbling to Teresa about something. The optician forced his face into an unwilling smile and greeted him professionally. The old man was slightly deaf and the pitch of his voice grated.

He talked incessantly through his tonometry test as the optician tried to measure the pressure inside his eyes.

'Puff of air coming now, Mr Abate.'

He picked up his ophthalmoscope and moved closer to Mr Abate. 'Try and hold still for me, Mr Abate,' he said gently. 'I'm just trying to get a look at your optic nerve to check it's as healthy as the rest of you.'

But the old man grumbled on. Not a single repeat booking in his brother's hotel. First time ever since they'd started up the place thirty-five years back that clients had checked out at the reception desk and hadn't immediately asked to reserve the same room for next year. Too worried, they'd said. Too worried that they might swim into a dead body! Damned migrants were turning this paradise island into a horror story!

The optician drew back his head and let his own eyes close briefly. The vein above his right ear throbbed. As he opened his eyes, he saw that Teresa was standing diagonally on the threshold of the shop, her left hand flat against her ear to block out Mr Abate. She was doing that chewing and pursing thing with her mouth that he knew meant tears.

A few years back, continued Mr Abate undeterred, his brother's hotel had had a waiting list as long as your arm for rooms; now the reservation book was as blank as you like. Damn migrants were ruining Lampedusa; everyone was choosing Sardinia these days for their holidays, although they all knew they'd get fleeced over there. Price of a pedalo in Sardinia was double what he charged here in August. More than double! Driven away trade, those migrants, they'd driven away trade.

The optician could smell mackerel on the old man's breath. He was careful always to clean his own teeth after lunch.

'Eyes wide open now, Mr Abate, please.'

Got to stop everyone talking about the migrants, Mr Abate droned on. That's the problem, you see. Everyone's focus is on the migrants. Every concert held on the island is a fund-raiser for the migrants, every newspaper story that mentions Lampedusa is about the migrants. Well, it's time to change the record!

'All looking good, Mr Abate,' soothed the optician as one hand clenched into a fist behind his back. Teresa was still on the doorstep. Her neck was flushed and her chin was tilted upwards. He was reminded of the girl in the turquoise T-shirt who had been too proud to cry on the boat.

He cleared his throat. 'Now I'd like to test your peripheral vision quickly,' he said courteously. 'Could you please concentrate on the light spots I'm going to show you and call out when you see one?'

Not even our problem, muttered the old man as he positioned himself forward in the chair. Not even our problem and yet everywhere you look, they're in your face.

'It's important you tell me when you see the light spots, Mr Abate.'

What's it got to do with us anyway? What have any of these people got to do with us?

'Mr Abate? The light spots!'

A door slammed and they both jumped at the loud bang. The optician looked up sharply and was just in time to see Teresa run past the window in the direction of Giulia's shop, her face beetroot-red from suppressed crying. He took off his glasses and massaged his eyes, breathing out slowly. She must have forgotten that Giulia and Gabriele had left Lampedusa last week.

'What was that?' said Mr Abate, fumbling on the table for his glasses. 'What the hell was that?'

The optician pushed his own glasses back onto the bridge of his nose and rubbed his hands together. 'Just the wind, Mr Abate,' he said reassuringly as he steered the old gentleman's head back towards the chin-rest. 'Just the wind.'

Chapter 12

If the wind had picked up. If the wind had not stayed soft. If the wind had begun to needle the sea until it raged in fury. If.

How many times had he tortured himself with the 'if' game over the last twelve months? A year on and he still played it at night in his head when he could not sleep; he played it staring at his computer in the office; he played it walking to the post office; he played it in the waiting room at the airport. And it played him. Over and over.

If the wind had suddenly picked up, Francesco would have called the shop to warn it would be an uncomfortable cruise with the sea so choppy. Best to postpone until next week, he would have said. If he had tripped on that loose paving stone on Via Roma on the run home and had sprained his ankle, he could not have boarded a boat on crutches. If Maria had not phoned about going out for dinner and instead he had chanced his luck with the last of the sardines at the fishmonger's, perhaps he and Teresa would both have had terrible food poisoning and he would have called Francesco from his bed to make their excuses. If he had not boarded that boat on that day, he would have spent the weekend marking down last season's sunglasses and setting up a sale. Now, a full year on, he might have made a little profit and perhaps he would be surprising his boy by putting a few hundred euros into his account to help with the launch of his new business. The circles beneath his eyes would not be bruised by dark shadows, he would sleep easily at night, and his wife would not wake up screaming, unable to breathe. If.

Wait! He is not the only player in this game. What about them, whispers the voice in his head? Where does this new narrative leave the refugees and their waving hands? If he had not boarded that boat on that day, they would still have boarded theirs. They would still have capsized and ended up in the water. So look! There they are in the waves screaming, and yet now there is no one to hear them. They're waving and they're clutching at hands that are not there. Hands that will not come, hands that will never come because they're busy dialling Mrs Maggiorani to remind her of her sight test next week and busy putting sale stickers on the ladies' sunglasses.

No. The cards had been dealt out already and there would be no reshuffling of the pack. He would accept his hand and play it out; he would not choose to sit out the game and simply watch. It was just that sometimes he wished his head could be still again, the way it had been before they took the boat trip. When his thoughts were not constantly rising and falling like the swell of the sea, searching for answers, continually tossing questions and flinging ifs and buts at him until he wanted to weep with exhaustion. Because you know, if he had only . . .

For pity's sake! He turned on the cold tap at the sink and stuck his face under the icy stream until his breath came in gasps. Get over yourself, he muttered as he searched for the towel. Get over yourself because you are where you are. And anyway, he reminded himself as he picked up his razor – today being the first anniversary of the shipwreck – it could be a good day as well as a sad day. It would be a good day because three of those refugees they had rescued were coming back to the island and they would see each other again. He checked his watch. In two hours they would be reunited. Less than two hours. He felt a tide of excitement and nerves knot in his stomach.

Was that Teresa singing? The optician put down his razor curiously and opened the bathroom door a little, putting his ear to the crack. Yes, it was definitely Teresa's voice accompanying Madonna on the radio in the bedroom opposite. He peered through the little gap. He could see her now too, as she was making the bed, plumping up the pillows in time to the beat, dancing a little. There was lightness in her movements, almost joy.

'La la la, la la la la la . . .'

He smiled and shut the door quickly before she realized she was being watched and became self-conscious. Let her have a carefree moment! This last year had taken its toll on her; the nightmares had haunted her through the winter and her appetite had deserted her. But she'd begun to pick up considerably when Maria and Gabriele and Giulia had reappeared at the start of the new season, along with the warm weather. Occasionally he still woke up to her scrabbling at the sheets, unable to draw breath, and he knew then that she was in the water with them again, struggling to stay afloat. But during the summer her laugh had come back and now she was singing.

'La la la, la la la la la!'

Of course, the tune was inane. How did people get paid for such preposterous rubbish? He was surprised when he picked up his razor again to realize he was also singing it. He grinned foolishly. At least Matteo hadn't witnessed that!

He trimmed the little salt-and-pepper goatee beard he now wore. He still had the dark rings under his eyes and his face was decidedly thinner. He had lost weight over the year; those beige trousers he'd bought towards the end of last summer hung on him now; Teresa said he looked liked he'd borrowed his father's trousers. Yet he still felt strong, especially on a day like today. He shrugged back his shoulders and flexed the muscles in his chest. He must keep calm and keep his emotions under control. He needed to manage this properly for Teresa's sake. Pushing open the bathroom door, he was startled by her pirouetting across the landing. They both laughed.

It was a greyish morning and the sky was surly, but it was still warm enough to sit outside on the café terrace. Almost as soon as they sat down, Maria, Matteo and Francesco arrived, and the optician could feel a swell of excitement rise up in him. Francesco had spent the last three days working like a dog on the boat, touching up her paintwork, washing salt stains from her cushion covers, scrubbing the sea slime off her fenders. Now the old girl was ready, said Francesco, to welcome them like kings. That afternoon, the eight of them would take a few of the survivors back on the water to the spot of the shipwreck. There would be a ceremony to remember those they could not save. Maria had bought flowers to throw into the sea; she told them her kitchen was alight with the yellow and white blooms.

It wasn't that he was nervous about being on the water; he was a man of the sea, for pity's sake, salt water was in his blood! He had sailed countless times since the shipwreck, both here and back in Naples. He'd helmed yachts; he'd been out on pleasure cruisers, and this summer he and Francesco had often taken *Galata* on fishing trips to the cove off Rabbit Beach. OK, he would admit he scanned the waves a little more attentively than before, but he had never felt panicked or anything. Today, though, would be the first time that all eight of them would be back out there together. All eight on board *Galata*. And under the excitement there was an unsettling sense of a portent. He began to fold and unfold his paper napkin. There was just this feeling that history might choose to repeat itself somehow, a fear that the sea might decide to throw them another challenge.

He tore the napkin down the middle. He must be going soft! It was enough that he'd been singing along to Madonna this morning: was he going to become superstitious now too?

Giulia and Gabriele arrived with Elena in tow. Elena craned her neck to look at the pastries displayed on the counter inside and wandered in to make a more informed choice. The optician glanced at his watch again and warned them they would not have time to linger over their coffee now if they were to get to the town hall by 10.30. It was like when they saw them at the airport hangar for the memorial service: they needed to be there at the moment of their arrival so they would know that the friends were anxious to see them; that all these months they had been waiting for them. He said nothing, but his left leg trembled nervously under the table.

Francesco was talking about the conference that was to be held at the town hall before the ceremony at sea; it was a conference, he explained, to look at what had been learnt from the tragedy. Elena and Giulia said they'd be interested to sit in on it, but the optician screwed up his face in distaste. He shied away from such public gatherings. It was all hot air anyway and it would just irritate him and get him worked up. A roomful of official bleeding hearts from Italy and the EU saying how awful it was that shipwrecks were still occurring, shaking their heads over last month's tragedy that had seen some 500 people drowned off the coast of Malta. Yes, it was awful – so what were they actually doing about it? He drummed his fingers on the table. It had been barely a year since the Italian Navy had launched its special search-and-rescue mission, Operation Mare Nostrum, and already the government was announcing its closure, saying it was too costly to run without the help of its European neighbours. No, it was best he didn't attend the conference. He could not stomach any more of their empty promises. Teresa put a hand on his jiggling knee to still him.

He took a deep breath. Anyway, this was to be a happy day, a day for celebration! Elena had bought a selection of cakes and sweet biscuits and was pressing them on the group. She dug him in the ribs. 'You could do with fattening up a bit,' she teased him, proffering the plate.

He studied the cakes carefully and selected a small almond biscuit. It was still warm from the oven and crumbled in his mouth, making him cough. They laughed at him as the tears rolled down his cheeks.

Maria had brought the letter they had all received from the town hall with the programme of events. The survivors and some of the relatives of the dead had arrived on the island last night, she read aloud, having met the Pope in Rome. After the conference this morning there would be a light lunch and then the special ceremony would take place with a flotilla of boats making a pilgrimage to the site. He grimaced at that. Call him selfish, but he wished they could filter out all these official engagements and just enjoy the private moments with the survivors alone. He knew the others felt the same; he could see Gabriele scowling. Francesco looked up at the sky and clicked his tongue disapprovingly. There would be rain later, he warned. You could feel it coming.

He took Teresa's arm on the way to the town hall and squeezed it against his. He needed this reunion to be healing for her. He hoped it would be healing for all of them. Just in front of the mayor's office, they met some friends of Elena's from a local NGO who were planning a demonstration. He looked at their placards and leaned down to see the half-furled banners they had made from old sheets.

Inside the town hall their names were ticked off a long list by a harassed employee who kept dropping her pen as she tried to leaf through the pages on her clipboard. She motioned to the heavy oak door on her right. Everyone is in there, she said, in that room.

The optician was nearest the door. He hesitated, his fingers curled around the handle, his heart pounding. He turned and looked at his friends as his hand pushed down. Their faces were charged with excitement and fear and he saw that they all needed this to be a success as much as he did. How ironic that they had come to need so much from these refugees who had nothing! Sometimes in his dreams, the hands he saw waving now in the water were white, not black at all. He nodded at his friends. The door handle was depressed but still he could not quite push the door open. It was Teresa who thrust it wide in the end.

The room was small and full of middle-aged white men in suits and young East Africans wearing T-shirts, jeans and trainers. Beside the long trestle table at the back of the room, which was laid with jugs of fruit juice and coffee urns, the optician spotted one of the fishermen who had helped *Galata* with the rescue. He was spruced up in a brown corduroy jacket, his red hand huge on the little espresso cup he was holding. But the optician did not have time to observe more.

The young man, the first one they had rescued, was in Teresa's arms almost instantaneously and they hugged each other like a mother and son. After a few seconds, the boy pulled away from her, chattering excitedly, wanting to show her something.

'Look!' he said, cuddling a piece of material to his chin like a child with a comforter. 'Look!'

The optician recognized it immediately. It was the bright pink T-shirt that Teresa had given the young man when he had been dragged naked aboard *Galata*, the one he had worn like a pair of pants. Teresa cupped the teenager's face in her hands. How humbling that this boy should have kept it, that after all this time and after God knows how many refugee camps and asylum centres, he still had it! He had treasured Teresa's kindness. She pulled the boy to him quickly so he should not see her weep.

Maria and Gabriele were exclaiming over a piece of paper that the other two refugees had given them. The eldest of the survivors, a man perhaps in his early thirties, had learnt a few words of Italian and explained to them that they had wanted to bring a gift for the people who had saved their lives. It was not much, he said with a little shrug of embarrassment, but it had been done – he touched his heart – with all their love. The optician bent over the paper. It was a simple but beautifully executed drawing of a grasping hand coming out of the water and being met above by another hand which clasped it in a fierce grip. It was the summary of their history.

The eldest survivor, they learnt over coffee, had been a teacher in Eritrea. It was not a good job, he made them understand, to teach children who had no future. Through his limited Italian and their poor English they pieced and cobbled together the refugees' stories; it was like doing a difficult crossword puzzle with everyone chipping in and guessing the answers to the clues. The optician had to concentrate hard to follow. He grasped that all three survivors were living in Sweden now, that most of those who had been rescued were living there, waiting for their asylum claims to be processed so that they would be able to work and start new lives. They were a little frustrated that their lives were on pause while the paperwork went through. Sweden was beautiful and very cold, they were saying, but they were not complaining.

He cut across them with an apologetic wave of his hand. What about the girl? he asked eagerly. What had happened to the girl, the girl in the turquoise T-shirt? The three men conferred among themselves for a moment in their own language. Norway, they suggested? Maybe Norway? He felt his shoulders sink.

The woman with the clipboard came into the room and made an announcement that the conference would start shortly. Francesco explained to the three men that they would see them at the port for the ceremony at sea, reassuring them that he would take them in his boat, that they would all be together. The young man who was still clutching Teresa's T-shirt shuffled nervously from foot to foot, chewing his lip. He was very frightened, the other two explained. He almost had not come because he was so scared of being at sea again. The optician took the teenager's hand, balled it into a fist, clasped his own on top of it and then pointed towards the drawing. The boy looked for a second or two into the optician's eyes as if searching for something, and then his face relaxed. He nodded at the optician, trusting him.

It was late afternoon by the time they cast off and the sky was still unsure whether to dump its heavy rainclouds or not. The optician scanned it suspiciously. Maria and Teresa were sitting on a bench on deck, each holding a hand of the nervous young man. The first time he had taken Teresa out to sea after the shipwreck, she had been white and seasick. Now, fussing over this boy she had helped save, she just looked content. He began to relax too.

The teacher had stopped talking almost as soon as he had boarded *Galata*. He had moved towards the prow of the boat, where he stood with his face to the wind, staring straight ahead. The other young man, his baseball cap pulled low over his forehead, was sitting beside the lifebuoy, one hand raised and stroking its coiled rope. The optician nudged his foot with his own and gave him the thumbs-up sign. The young man returned the gesture with a small smile.

On each side of *Galata* the coastguard and fishing vessels flanked them, rocking her a little.

He felt shame when they reached the shipwreck site – shame and indignation that they were so ludicrously close to shore. The point of the coastline looked vulgar jutting out into the sea like that. He imagined how the shoreline must have taunted the migrants while they were drowning in the water, flaunting its proximity and parading the promise of its harbour. They were barely a kilometre from land and yet 368 people had died here. He covered his face with his hands and felt Gabriele grip his shoulder.

The coastguard vessel gave two long blasts on its horn, the sign that the ceremonies should begin. *Galata*'s crew had not planned anything specific themselves, although it was understood that if anyone would speak, it must be Francesco. But the optician saw that the three survivors had rehearsed what they should do. Each of them picked up a bouquet of Maria's sunny flowers and turned to face the water. They began to pray in their own language, half chanting, half singing, steadying themselves against the sea's gait with one hip lodged between the bars of the gunwale. Then, with a cry, they threw the flowers into the sea and the optician saw the eldest survivor take something that looked like coarse sand or perhaps rice from his jeans pocket and distribute it between them. They recited some more verses together and scattered the grains onto the waves, their heads bowed.

He watched their backs convulsing with sobs, and again he

was reminded of them at the aircraft hangar in their pitiful second-hand, cast-off clothes and ill-matched shoes. He saw the gleaming coffins, spaced out with military precision, the cheerful teddies propped up on the tiny white caskets, the girl with her blistered fingers and the stink of her burnt-out, ruined life. And he saw the young man wearing Teresa's pink T-shirt bunched around his waist like a nappy, howling like a helpless new-born, slithering onto the deck in his afterbirth of oil and gasoline.

The same young man turned from the sea and faced him, holding out his hand.

'Come,' he said, looking him squarely in the eye. 'Come and be with us.'

So they joined hands – all of them – and stood in a line, looking out across the sea. And when the refugees began to pray again, he did not feel uncomfortable. His right hand held the teenager's and in his left he clutched Teresa's hand. He no longer saw the coastguard and the press boats and the fishing vessels that surrounded them. He just felt them and only them, and stillness. He could feel the collective pulse of them all, his dearest friends and these refugees, throbbing in his own wrists. He could feel their shared lifeline.

The teenager turned to him, let go of his hand and held up his index finger. Today, he said, I am one year old. He pointed to the optician and then to the sea. In there, he was trying to say, jabbing his finger at the water, I was dead. But here – he swept his arms across *Galata*'s deck – here, I was reborn.

The first spots of rain were falling as they got back to port. This time, though, when the three survivors climbed down onto the quayside there were no tears at saying goodbye; tomorrow afternoon they would see each other again and no one would try to stop them meeting. So they parted with smiles and bear hugs, sure of each other, like family. But he still watched as they wandered away until he saw that they had met up with the other survivors and were safe.

It was pretty much dark by the time they'd sorted out *Galata* and fixed her back safely at her mooring. Gabriele said he needed a beer. Matteo replied that he needed several. That's when the rain came, rupturing all its clouds on them at once and forcing them to run for cover. And that's why the optician ended up in that awful bar he hated, with the crude electric lighting and the irritating music.

The first beer quickly became two. And then, when the optician checked his watch, it turned out to be very much *aperitivo* time and it would be a crime really not to raise a glass of wine to the day.

What was that song they were playing? Was it that Madonna track? He nudged Teresa.

'La la la,' he mimed and they both started laughing.

'You're more chilled,' said Maria, giving his knee a fond squeeze. 'Did you know that, Mr Fastidiousness? You're more chilled these days.'

He sent the wine back to make a point.

A few wispy clouds lingered in the night sky when they left the bar, veiling the moon in a sheer film. There was no wind as such to shift the clouds. The optician felt the alcohol swirl pleasantly around his brain as he tipped his head back to stare at the stars.

Maria linked arms with him. He offered his left arm to Teresa, who in turn held out her left elbow to Francesco. The optician grinned as Giulia threaded her arm under Francesco's sleeve and snaked her right hand into Matteo's coat pocket. They walked like that, towards Via Roma, as a human chain, arm in arm and laughing wildly. Just the eight of them. Just the eight.

'Hey,' he said, nudging his hip into Maria's and looking across Teresa to Francesco. 'If the wind stays soft, how about we take *Galata* out tomorrow night so we can wake up to a sunrise on the water on Sunday morning? An October mini-break?'

A murmur of approval waved from one end of the line to the other.

'Just the eight of us,' said the optician. 'If the wind stays soft.'

Epilogue

You ask me why I don't give interviews. You ask me why I don't like to tell this story. But if I still cannot believe it really happened, how can you? If I talk about it, your jaw will drop and you will say, but how did you, how could you? It is impossible for you to understand. Only the eight of us can really understand. You see, we were eight on that boat. Just eight. With one rubber ring.

I saw them every day and yet I did not see them. I did not reach out. Not until that day on the sea when I was confronted for the first time in my life with so many people in great need – in the greatest need of all – did I stretch out my hand.

Forty-seven. We saved forty-seven. But we couldn't save them all.

I was never trying to be a hero. I'm humbled by what happened on the water. I'm humbled. Whenever I have a tough period now in my life, I always go back to that scene on the sea. In my hands I feel again the grip of those naked, desperate people who were so close to the end. And I say to myself: you have a little house, you have your little business, you have a little family. You are not in the water.

Because I cannot forget those fingers that cemented into mine. Nor those hands that slipped away.

That's when the nightmares crawl back. The oily, slippery hands vanishing under the water, the animalistic screams that were not seagulls, muffled, then swallowed by the waves. We are all haunted by them.

I was on the sea that day. And I don't rule out that it could be me on the sea again tomorrow. There will be another time, another boat. There will be more hands, more bodies thrashing, more voices begging. Every time I am on the sea now, I'm searching for them, scouring, breathless.

Acknowledgements

I would like to thank the optician of Lampedusa, Carmine Menna and his wife Rosaria for their trust in me and for agreeing to speak to me about the most difficult day of their lives. Their story haunts me and their courage inspires me.

Thank you also to Alessandra Maggiorani, who first introduced me to the optician and who has followed this journey so patiently all the way through.

This book started as a report for BBC Radio 4's *PM* programme, and my thanks go to Eddie Mair, Jo Carr and Emma Rippon, who have always championed the optician's story. I am so grateful to the Prix Bayeux Calvados, which recognizes international war reporting, for highlighting my report and bringing it to the attention of my brilliant French editor Jeanne Pham Tran, whom I thank for her vision, hard work and encouragement. Likewise my Penguin editor, Josephine Greywoode, and all the team at Penguin for their unwavering belief that the optician's story needed to be told.

Thank you to those who helped me with the research for this book, particularly optometrist Rajeev Kurani, Gaim Kibreab, Efrem Gebreab and members of the Holy Redeemer Eritrean Catholic Gheez-Rite Chaplaincy in East Acton.

My thanks to my dearest friends Janet Skeslien Charles and Sam Upton who ploughed through my first drafts with such enthusiasm, dedication and incisiveness: I owe you both so much.

And, of course, my thanks to Denis Bernard for supporting me throughout and for always believing in me and this book. Likewise my wonderful parents and my A. B. – your positive energy and love have always carried me through.